Praise for T. J. Phillips's debut
Joe Wilder mystery,

DANCE OF THE MONGOOSE...

"Engaging . . . different and distinctive."
—*Kirkus Reviews*

"A sensual novel of misplaced passions and forgotten dreams."
—FAYE KELLERMAN,
bestselling author of *Sanctuary*

"Phillips competently weaves a modern tale of greed, betrayal and thwarted love."
—*Publishers Weekly*

"What more could you want. An exotic location, an intriguing puzzle, mysterious characters, and an engaging, if reluctant, detective. In *Dance of the Mongoose*, T. J. Phillips delivers all of this and more."
—PETER ROBINSON,
award-winning author of *Innocent Graves*

Berkley Prime Crime Books by T. J. Phillips

DANCE OF THE MONGOOSE
WOMAN IN THE DARK

WOMAN
in the
DARK

T.J. Phillips

BERKLEY PRIME CRIME, NEW YORK

WOMAN IN THE DARK

A Berkley Prime Crime Book / published by arrangement with
the author

PRINTING HISTORY
Berkley Prime Crime hardcover edition / February 1997
Berkley Prime Crime mass-market edition / December 1997

The Putnam Berkley World Wide Web site address is
http://www.berkley.com

ISBN: 0-425-16110-2

Berkley Prime Crime Books are published
by The Berkley Publishing Group,
a member of Penguin Putnam Inc., 200 Madison Avenue,
New York, NY 10016.
The name BERKLEY PRIME CRIME and the BERKLEY PRIME CRIME
design are trademarks belonging to Berkley Publishing Corporation.

PRINTED IN THE UNITED STATES OF AMERICA

10 9 8 7 6 5 4 3 2 1

Author's Note

The title of this novel and several of the chapter titles are inspired by the 1941 Broadway musical *Lady in the Dark* by Moss Hart (book), Kurt Weill (music), and Ira Gershwin (lyrics).

Pre-Eleven

It began a few weeks ago, with a phone call from Jenny Hughes, but I am not going to start there. That call, an invitation to dinner, was my first scene, my entrance into the drama, but it was not the true beginning; far from it. The story had been going on for quite some time. So I won't begin with me. I have decided, in light of what we now know about it, to preface my own involvement with the account of a house, and the family who lived there, and what happened there one rainy night sixteen years ago.

I am a novelist, and in publishing this would be described as a prologue. But I am also a playwright, and in the theater this scene is known as a curtain-raiser, or pre-eleven. That odd phrase has its roots in the printed scripts of plays. The first scene, Act One, Scene One, is notated thus: "1-1." Any action or tableau, or whatever, that the director chooses as an opening image for the production—the first thing the audience sees when the curtain rises—is referred to as pre-1-1, or, in the theatrical shorthand that has evolved, pre-eleven. I have chosen to present this case in theatrical terms because from the beginning there was a distinct air of artifice, unreality, *staginess* about it.

So, the house. The northern coast of Long Island, eu-
phemistically known as the Gold Coast in honor of the
mansions that line it and the rich people who live in them.
This particular mansion looms up from a low promontory
above a beach at the end of a long, tree-lined drive. It is
in the curve of Cold Spring Harbor, almost exactly between
the town of that name and Oyster Bay. I have seen this
house, so I can describe it: it is huge, yellow, and rather
hideous.

It was built in the late teens or early twenties of this
century by a family with a famous last name that can only
be described as *nouveau riche*. Their taste, or lack of it,
tended toward the Spanish influence popular at that time.
The big, square, two-story, yellow stucco building is replete
with little black wrought-iron balconies along the upstairs
rooms, and the sloping roof is of corrugated red clay tile.
There are fourteen rooms and six bathrooms in the house,
which includes a basement apartment for three servants; a
housekeeper, a butler who would double as chauffeur and/
or gardener, and a maid. The front entrance is arched, with
big black carriage lamps flanking the doorway and Spanish
columns lining the red flagstone porch. On the right side
of the house, if you are facing it, a curved glass enclosure
filled with exotic green plants juts out into the yard: con-
servatories were all the rage in the Jazz Era. On the left is
a four-car garage, and beyond the trees to the left of that
is a swimming pool, complete with sundeck and lounge
chairs and a pool house that is used primarily as a guest
cottage. A small forest separates the property from the main
road, and the driveway ends in a big circle in front of the
house. There is a large, ornate, faux-Roman fountain in the
center of the circle, and the wide green lawns surrounding
it are dotted with statuary: nude nymphs and satyrs. Behind
the main house is a patio surrounded by the lawn that ends
at the low stone wall along the edge of the cliff. Stone steps
lead down from there to the beach. The view of Long Island
Sound is spectacular.

Inside the house is a different matter. The family that constructed this pseudo-Spanish/faux-Roman nightmare lost their considerable fortune in the stock market crash of 1929, and the house with it. It was sold to Bradley Masterson, the kitchen appliance king. He had vague ideas of tearing down the house and building something else on the property. This never happened: the house stood vacant throughout the thirties, and in 1941 Masterson gave it to his son, Bradley Junior, and his bride, Sarah, as a wedding present.

Sarah was the daughter of well-to-do New Yorkers from Manhattan's Upper East Side, and she naturally possessed that flair the famous upstarts who built the place never had. To the surprise of no one, her first act on moving into the house was completely redecorating. Every stick of furniture, fixture, carpet, and painting was removed, replaced by newer, better things, but she left the wrought iron and the fountain and the statues because they amused her. The interior has been redone a couple of times since then, of course, but the people responsible, like Sarah Masterson, have known a thing or two about decoration. To this day, the quiet good taste inside the house vies with the silly exterior.

Sarah was pregnant by the time Bradley Junior went off to fight in Europe, and she was a widow by the time their daughter, Laura, was born. She never remarried, and she continued to live in the house, watching as Laura grew from a beautiful child to a beautiful young woman. Masterson *père* died in 1955, and when his wife followed him in 1957, she left Masterson Appliances, which is now Masterson Electronics, to her granddaughter.

Laura Masterson was just fifteen when one of America's largest manufacturers of refrigerators, ranges, and dishwashers was bequeathed to her. She was a tall, graceful blond girl with big blue eyes and a honeyed complexion that darkened beautifully when she went to the beach, which was often. Her only child status did nothing to deter her from becoming the most popular teenager on the North Shore. The house on the promontory was the site of frequent parties, and her gang of girlfriends and string of boyfriends all adored her. I understand she loved to dance, and her favorite singer was Elvis Presley. She had a passion for Broadway musicals. She also enjoyed reading: her favorite book was *Madame Bovary*, a fact which is rather ironic in light of subsequent events. Later, at Stanton College, she majored in English. She wrote an apparently brilliant term paper on Gustave Flaubert, and she was the president of her sorority and her class valedictorian, so we know that she was smart, in addition to being rich and beautiful.

When she was twenty-one, Laura Masterson met Walter Vale, an up-and-coming executive at Masterson Appliances who was eight years her senior. He was handsome and fun and athletic, and she was immediately attracted. Though not exactly a virgin by that point, she apparently found their sex life to be rather wonderful, too. With much friendly orchestrating from her mother, she accepted Walter's inevitable proposal. Sarah Masterson gave them the house, as it had been given to her upon her marriage, and moved into New York City, to a penthouse apartment on Fifth Avenue.

By all accounts, Laura and Walter were very happy at the beginning of their marriage. Walter was immediately elevated to vice-president, and he assumed the presidency of the appliance company ten years later, shortly before the merger that resulted in Masterson Electronics. The couple soon had two daughters, Emma (named after Laura's favorite heroine) and Sarah (named after Laura's mother).

Walter was delighted with his daughters, but he secretly longed for a son. When Laura became pregnant a third time, he silently crossed his fingers, but it was not to be. This pregnancy was ectopic, and Laura was soon stricken with great pain and rushed to the hospital. She survived the operation, but there would be no more children.

If Emma and Sarah were slightly spoiled little girls, this could explain it. Their parents, particularly their mother,

lavished on them the affection that had been planned for
several children. The two girls were brought up in the Spanish house above the Sound, and they were fifteen and
twelve years old, respectively, on the night sixteen years
ago when Laura Masterson Vale was murdered.

I remember the incident from the newspaper and television reports at the time. I had recently graduated from college, and I'd just moved to New York City, where I was
already at work on what would eventually become my first
produced play. The case was quite a scandal, as it involved
sex, drugs, and a famous family. For weeks it was all everyone in New York was discussing. I can only recreate it here
based on what I have read about it, and on what I have
been told.

There is a temptation to begin with that most obvious of
openings: *It was a dark and stormy night.* I won't, but it
happens to be true. The thunderstorm hit Long Island at
about seven o'clock in the evening, as the Vale family was
gathering in the dining room, and continued throughout the
night of September 14–15. The crashing thunder and the
pounding rain and the howling wind would later be described as a form of evidence: it was given as the reason
Walter Vale took the sleeping pill, and the reason everyone
in the house claimed not to have heard anything.

The testimony at the subsequent inquest included all sorts
of extraneous details, such as the fact that Rock Cornish
hen was the main dish of the meal Walter and Laura and
their two daughters were served that night. There was a
salad first, and the chicken was accompanied by wild rice
and string beans *almondine*. Walter and Laura consumed a
bottle of chardonnay between them, and the children had
water. Dinner was followed by vanilla ice cream with chocolate sauce. Afterward, Walter and Laura went into the living room for coffee and their habitual evening conversation.
The two girls went immediately up to their bedrooms.
School had begun the week before, and they had homework
assignments.

There were two servants at the time, but only the maid, a young woman named Hannah Melton, lived in the basement apartment. The housekeeper/cook, Mrs. Erwin, came in daily and went home as soon as the Vales' dinner was ready. There had not been a manservant in residence since the old days, when domestic service was still considered an honorable profession for men.

Hannah cleared the dining room table, served coffee to Walter and Laura, cleaned up in the kitchen, and was in the basement in time for her favorite television program at ten o'clock. At eleven she went to bed. The storm—and any other noises—could not be heard from there, and she slept through the night undisturbed.

Fifteen-year-old Emma was the lovely, blond, blue-eyed image of her mother, and she had just entered the tenth grade at the local private high school. According to her testimony, she remained in her room all evening, solving algebra problems and reading three chapters of *The Scarlet Letter* for a quiz the next day. Sarah, the twelve-year-old whose darker hair and eyes and rather round face resembled Walter more than Laura, filled in some pages of a grammar book and listened to her new cassette of her favorite rock group. Both children were in bed by ten, as was the rule of the house on school nights, and their mother came briefly into their rooms to say goodnight. Little Sarah remembered Laura closing the curtains near her bed and drawing the blanket closer around her as the thunder crashed outside and the rain pelted the windows. Then she kissed her younger daughter on the forehead and left the room.

Back downstairs, according to Walter Vale, he and his wife chatted for about forty-five minutes, and Laura made two phone calls. She called her mother in New York every night at about ten-thirty. She spoke briefly with Sarah Masterson, then called her friend, Annemarie Nevins, to talk about a luncheon one of their charities was hosting in two weeks time. She was still on the phone with her friend at a quarter to eleven, when Walter went upstairs for his nightly ritual: a hot shower and the eleven o'clock news on the television in the master bedroom. On this night, he said, he took a sleeping pill. He had to be up and in the city early the next morning, and he didn't want the thunder keeping him awake. According to his testimony, he turned off the television at eleven-thirty and was asleep within five minutes. Laura, as usual, remained downstairs.

The hour or two after Walter retired every night was Laura's time alone, and she used it to record events of her day in the diary she had kept throughout her adult life. Walter had an office next to the living room, but she had a desk in the corner of the living room by a picture window. She would sit here every evening with her coffee, gazing out at the Sound and writing in her private journal. This diary, some of which was later made public, confirms that she did so that night. But because of the rain, she would not have had much of a view.

What happened next had never been made clear. It had to do with the private woman Laura Masterson Vale was, the woman even her family didn't seem to know. I've seen photographs of her, and she was certainly beautiful. On that night, September 14, she was a mere three weeks away from her thirty-ninth birthday, with forty looming large. Her marriage to Walter, according to the diary, had settled by that time into a comfortable, rather mechanical coexistence. Her life at this point was one of charity luncheons, of bridge and golf and tennis, of PTA meetings, of summer clothes and winter coats for the children, of dentists and dinner menus and shopping at Foodtown.

But she had always been romantic. She loved to dance, and she loved Broadway musicals and Elvis Presley, and her favorite novel was *Madame Bovary*. I'm not trying to excuse her; I'm simply trying to understand her.

I try to imagine her as she must have been that night, how she must have been feeling. The thoughts that must have raced through her mind as she sat at her little desk, straining her ears to check for sounds from upstairs. When

she was satisfied that all was silent in the house, she must
have stood up and hurried over to the closet in the foyer
near the front door. She put on her beige London Fog
trench coat over her low-cut, long-sleeved, clinging white
crêpe de chine dress and grabbed a black Totes umbrella.
She then slipped silently across the front hall, through the
kitchen and the utility room to the garage. She made her
way past the three cars and two bicycles. By the time she
emerged onto the sidewalk leading to the swimming pool,
she was probably running. Her loose, shoulder-length blond
hair and her pretty white slippers—so impractical in that
weather—would immediately have been soaked through.
With the winds reported from the Sound that night, I doubt
she made it ten feet with the umbrella: she probably closed
it as she ran. It was closed when it was found beside her
body the next day.

I can see her running now, sixteen years later, as if there
were a film of it before me. Her flight is lit by sudden
lightning and orchestrated by jarring crashes of thunder,
and there is, perhaps, a little smile on her lovely face as
she runs, thinking Heaven knows what thoughts in these,
the final moments of her life. She dashes pell-mell down
the sidewalk and across the redwood sundeck that rings the
pool and over the flagstones and through the open door of
the guest cottage, into the waiting arms of a young man
named Michael Trent.

Exactly what took place in the poolhouse was anybody's
guess, and it remained so for sixteen years. Laura Vale and
Michael Trent were found there at approximately twelve
forty-five the following afternoon. There were small,
matching, relatively bloodless entry wounds on the right
sides of their heads, just above the ears, and large, jagged
exit wounds on the other sides. It might have looked worse,
but the tiny pistol found clutched in Michael's right hand
was not very powerful. A nearly empty vial of cocaine was
found among the effects in a pocket of his jeans, and the
autopsy proved that he had ingested an impressive amount

of it in the hours before his death. No cocaine was found in Laura's system.

The official ruling was murder/suicide, the motive despair: in her diary that evening, Laura had recorded that tonight she was going to tell her lover that they would never see each other again. Trent was on the books as an unstable young man, with a history of alcohol and drug abuse. He had served a brief time in prison for assaulting a fellow lifeguard in Florida—in a dispute over a woman—and he was feared and loathed by the other employees at the private beach club in Oyster Bay where the Vales were members. The beach club where he had met Laura a year before.

It was a nine day wonder in every news medium in America at the time, and the same pictures, endlessly reproduced, entered everyone's consciousness. The photoportrait of Laura by Richard Avedon and the painting of her by Warhol. The beefcake nude shot of Trent, taken at a Florida beach party years before, always accompanied by the front-and-side-view mug shots of him from the Tampa Police Department. The tearful visage of Trent's mother, a Florida divorcée, at his otherwise unattended funeral. And, most of all, the stricken faces of Walter Vale and Sarah Masterson and the two young girls, Emma and Sarah, as the twelve-year-old placed a single white rose on her mother's polished ebony coffin.

I say that it was anybody's guess, but I know now that this isn't true. There was a witness to at least some of the events that night—but I'm getting ahead of myself. Laura Masterson Vale and Michael Trent died on that stormy night in September sixteen years ago. Having stated that, I will return to the present, to the beginning of my own involvement a few weeks ago.

To Jenny Hughes.

ONE

Jenny

I guess you could say she's the reason I got involved in the case. If it were not for her, I would never have become a detective. Of course, if it were not for her, I wouldn't be alive, either. I remind myself of that fact every time I see her, and I was thinking of it when I accepted her invitation for dinner.

She was sitting in the darkest, farthest corner of the restaurant. Not too crowded to begin with: a cold, rainy Sunday evening in late February, in one of those places that can only happen in Greenwich Village. Exposed brick walls, hammered tin ceiling, white linen tablecloths and napkins, candles and floral centerpieces, antique everything. Dim, indirect lighting, probably designed by theatrical specialists, creating an intimate atmosphere. A bejeweled, Lincoln Center Board of Directors–type dowager with her bank president-type husband at a table next to a girl with blue hair and a boy with a ring through his nose. Two attractive women at a front table, one a well-known actress, the other smiling as she records their conversation on a tiny machine on the table between them. Two attractive men at a corner table, holding hands, one of them a Pulitzer prize–winning playwright. Vivaldi playing softly in the background. A cup of coffee: $7.95. You've been there, right?

I dripped on the Something-or-other carpet as the red-vested waitperson of indeterminate gender led me to her table. I stopped briefly to say hello to my fellow playwright, whom I know slightly. I removed my coat and gloves and straightened my tie before dropping into the Louis the Something-or-other chair across from her. The waitperson— a girl, I now saw—took my coat and my order for ginger ale, and departed.

Her name is Jennifer Hughes, Jenny to her friends. She is, let's see, about thirty-two now. A rather small, very pretty Afro-Caribbean American, a native of St. Thomas, Virgin Islands. She was wearing a blue dress, and there was a glass of white wine on the table in front of her. She used to wear her hair cut very short in what was once called an Afro, but now it was longer, looser, and softer-looking around her face. Full, perfect lips and high cheekbones below enormous, dark eyes that bore an expression of surprising gravity. Her father, recently deceased, had been the governor of the Virgin Islands. The native man she almost married years ago was one of my two best friends in the world. I'm originally from St. Thomas, myself.

"Good evening, Joe," she said in her lovely voice, which bears the slightest trace of Calypso music and a fine finish of finishing school. "Thank you for coming."

I smiled. "Thanks for asking me."

She smiled, too, and reached for her wineglass. "You may change your mind when you hear why I asked you."

"Oh? Is something wrong?"

Jenny Hughes regarded me a moment, an unreadable expression on her serious face.

"Is something wrong?" she repeated. "I honestly don't know. I don't know what to make of it. But let's order first. Then I'll tell you."

We sat there across from each other, a beautiful black woman and a reasonably attractive white man who—this being the Village—raised fewer eyebrows than the punk couple and the two men holding hands, who raised none at all. The ginger ale arrived, and we were handed menus. Calligraphy on parchment.

This place was two blocks from the apartment I'd lived in for fifteen years, and I'd never been here before. It had never occurred to me to come here until Jenny called on Friday, two days before that night, and invited me to dinner, asking if I knew someplace nice near me. That left out the Greek diner and the pub with the dartboard that are my two regular haunts. I could imagine the Queen Mother in a diner faster than Jenny Hughes. So, here we were.

She ordered something French that turned out to be salmon, and I asked for chicken, because next to the word *poulet* I saw the word *artichaud*. I love artichokes.

For a few moments we regarded each other, sort of smiling across the table and listening to Vivaldi. I wasn't sure what to say to her. We have a history, she and I, and not a pleasant one. Painful memories on both sides, mostly hers. We weren't lovers, or anything like that, yet, in an odd way, what we'd been through together was even more intimate. Murder has a way of doing that. But that had all been seven years ago, and this was only the second time I'd seen her since then. The first was a couple of weeks before, when she came to my apartment and we cleared the air between us. I'd waited seven years for that interview.

Now, in the present, in the fancy, candlelit restaurant on a rainy Sunday night in Greenwich Village, she folded her hands on the table before her and leaned forward.

"How are you, Joe?" she asked.

I stared. How was I? Good question. I looked away across the room for a moment before replying, forming words in my mind. I decided in that moment that I was going to be perfectly honest with Jenny Hughes.

"Okay," I said at last. "I'm okay. I'm writing a new novel, and I have an idea for a new play. I belong to a health club, but I don't seem to get there as often as I'd like. My mother still lives on Fifth Avenue: I have dinner with her once a week. I see my sisters occasionally—I only see Lee when she comes up here on business." My sister Lee lives in St. Thomas with her husband. I haven't been back there since—well, seven years ago. "I'm thinking about buying a co-op. I occasionally date an actress friend when she's in New York, but she's usually in Hollywood with her TV series these days: she's a semi-regular on *Malibu Cop*. We aren't as serious as I think she'd like us to be, but it's open for discussion. I hang out with a couple of friends I've known since we all went to college together—"

"That's amazing!" Jenny cried.

I shrugged, smiling at her. "I don't know, it all sounds pretty dull to me. . . ."

"No, I mean you mentioning friends from college. That's what I want to talk to you about!"

I held up my hand to stop her as salads were lowered in front of us. "First, it's your turn. I've been doing all the talking here. How are *you* doing, Jenny?"

She did the same thing I'd done, sort of. She looked down at the table, ostensibly reaching for her salad fork but obviously forming an answer.

"I'm all right," she said. "I've taken an apartment in Gramercy Park, and I'm pretty much moved in. I'm still looking for something to do. You know, a job—a new profession, really."

"So, you've decided to stay in New York?" I asked.

She shrugged. "For a while, at least. I want to see how it goes, how I feel about it. I'm an island girl, really. The big city is quite a dramatic change of scenery. Now I'm just getting in touch with old friends up here and waiting for the rest of my new furniture to be delivered."

I nodded. When she'd arrived on my doorstep two weeks before, I was surprised to see her. She'd been living in St. Thomas with her recently widowed mother, Iris Hughes, last I'd heard. Jenny was—or had been—a teacher, first of

fourth graders and later of special children, those who were
mentally or emotionally challenged. But when she came to
see me, she informed me that her teaching career was behind her. Five or six years of working with problem children in a system that didn't give a damn about them—or
her—had been quite enough. That's what she'd told me,
anyway. But I wondered if, perhaps, the real reason was a
desire to get away from the Virgin Islands. Considering our
past experiences in St. Thomas, I wouldn't be surprised.

Her next words relieved me of all suspicion.

"I had to get out of there," she whispered, lifting her
gaze from the table directly into my eyes.

I nodded again. I wasn't going to follow that lead; not
now, at any rate. Later.

"So," I said, forcing a hearty smile as we both put down
our salad forks. "What's going on now? Why did you ask
me to dinner tonight?"

She leaned back in her chair. "Ah, yes. Well, you know
I went to college up here. Stanton. When I came to New
York two weeks ago, it was initially just going to be a visit.
The ten-year reunion of my graduating class. It was at the
Waldorf, last Saturday."

Stanton College is somewhere in the east Eighties, I remembered. Perhaps the best known of the non–Seven Sisters women's colleges, it was named for the woman who
practically invented modern feminism. Many important
women from famous families had been graduated from
Stanton, and it's still one of the best and most exclusive
schools around. Looking across the table at Jenny, I also
remembered that it was one of the first to accept minorities.
It was a logical choice for a well-to-do woman of color,
the daughter of a Virgin Islands senator who would later
be governor.

"How was the reunion?" I asked.

She reached for her wineglass. "Rather odd, as a matter
of fact. I mean, it was very nice, I suppose, and it was good
to see my college friends again, especially now that I plan

to live here. I was particularly glad to see my old room-mate, Emma—umm—Smith. Well, until she got me alone for a chat. Then I wasn't so sure. . . .'' She trailed off, shaking her head absently as she raised the glass to her lips.

"'Emma—umm—Smith'?" I quoted. "Just how close were you and your roommate? You seem to be having trouble remembering her name."

Jenny Hughes treated me to a dazzling smile. "Oh, she was my best friend there. It's just that she's married now, and I'm still getting used to calling her Emma Smith. In college she was Emma Vale."

I shrugged, waiting for her to continue.

She studied my face for a moment. "You don't recognize the name, do you? Emma Vale. Emma Masterson Vale."

"Emma Mas—" I began.

Then I got it. I leaned forward, staring, just as our entrées arrived. The waitress lowered a surprisingly small portion of chicken breast, artichoke hearts, and roasted new potatoes swimming in parsley butter before me. I waved away the inevitable peppermill, staring again as the girl retreated and Jenny picked up her fork.

"Yes," she said, cutting a small bite of pinkish fish. "Emma is the elder daughter of Laura Masterson Vale."

"Wow." I blinked, trying to remember what I could of the murder/suicide. "Laura was her mother, the woman who—"

"Yes, the woman who was killed by her crazy lover. Emma was fifteen at the time. I met her three years later, at Stanton. We were assigned a dorm room together in our freshman year, and we immediately liked each other. She made a point of introducing the shy girl from the Islands to all of her friends, and she defended me against—well, even in a place as liberal as Stanton there were snobs. You know, girls who didn't particularly like my type sullying their lily-white halls."

I felt the blood rush to my face. "You're kidding!"

"I wish I was kidding, but it was very real. And it was a bit of a shock for me, I can tell you. We never really had that sort of thing in the Islands. There were about three hundred women at Stanton at the time, and only twelve of us were not Caucasian. I know: I counted them—I mean, I counted *us*. And some of those debutantes were from the Deep South." She shrugged, dismissing it. "Emma was my champion. *Our* champion. I've always been grateful to her."

"I can understand that," I said. "So, now you've seen her again. Why did you say it was odd?"

She paused, staring down at her plate for a moment before placing her knife and fork on it and pushing it away from her. She'd eaten maybe three bites. I had yet to touch my chicken and artichokes.

"What was odd," she said, "was what she told me when she got me alone at the party, away from the others. Away from her husband." She picked up her wineglass and drained it. I finally started in on my dinner, waiting for her to tell me. "It's the reason I called you, Joe. Why I asked you here tonight. Two things. First, Emma's giving a dinner party this Friday, at her grandmother's apartment on Fifth Avenue. She invited me, and she told me to bring a date. I want you to come with me. I want you to meet her and her family."

I put down my utensils. "Sure, I'll come. Thank you— but why? I mean, why me?"

"That's the second thing," Jenny said. She signaled to the hovering waitress and raised her empty wineglass. The girl nodded and went over to the bar. We waited in silence until the fresh glass was placed before her. She raised it to her lips, sipped, and put it down.

"I was thinking about St. Thomas," she said at last. "About what happened to us there seven years ago. You know, the—the murders. You're the one who got to the bottom of it all, Joe. You're the one who solved it. I know you're not a policeman, or a detective, or anything like that.

But you *are* a writer, and you're obviously very observant. Maybe if you meet Emma, get to know her a little, you'll be able to—I don't know—to tell her who it is.''

I watched her, remembering St. Thomas and trying to follow her train of thought. I didn't know where all this was leading.

"Who *what* is?" I finally asked.

For the second time that evening, Jenny Hughes looked directly into my eyes. I was raising my fork to my mouth when she said it, plain and simple. The fork clattered back down onto my plate.

"Emma says somebody's trying to kill her."

My apartment on Hudson Street can politely be described as "cozy," but that's just New Yorkese for "too damn small." It is the front half of the top floor of a four-story townhouse. That means three flights of narrow stairs before you even get there, four if you count the front stoop—and as the out-of-breath husband in *Barefoot in the Park* observes, "I counted the stoop." Miniature living room and kitchenette, a postage stamp of a bathroom, and a bedroom that is exactly that—a room with a bed in it. You walk in the door and fall out the window, not enough room to change your mind; even the mice are round-shouldered: Neil Simon isn't the only wit to mine humor from Greenwich Village walk-ups.

I've been thinking about moving.

One asset my apartment *does* have is an actual, working fireplace, one of the three or four remaining in New York City. I threw one of those wax imitation logs on the grate and set it aflame when we came in, dripping from the downpour outside. Then I took the required one-and-a-half steps into the kitchen area and put Mr. Coffee to work. I searched the lone cabinet above the sink/range/refrigerator configuration for the bottle of brandy I was certain Donna had left there before taking off to be a Malibu policewoman. Jenny, at my insistence, sat in the "guest seat," the armchair near the fire, looking around her.

"Well," she said, "this certainly is cozy."

I laughed. "That's New Yorkese for 'too damn small,' but thank God for politicians' daughters." I found the brandy and—thank you, Donna—two actual snifters, and came over to join her. "Coffee will be served momentarily, and I have some Pepperidge Farm cookies around here somewhere. But first—" I poured the brandy and we clinked. "*Salüd.*"

"Thank you," she said.

"Thank *you* for dinner," I replied. I sat on the couch across from her, with the coffee table between us. "Now, tell me about Emma Vale."

She sipped her brandy and relaxed back into the armchair. The firelight, such as it was, gave a soft glow to her ebony face and hair. I watched her eyes: she was thinking, putting everything in some sort of order in her mind. After a while she began, her low voice clear in the quiet room, its only competition the occasional crackle of the log and the faint hiss from the radiator in the corner and the muffled sounds of rain against the windows and traffic out in Hudson Street. At some point I went to get the coffee and cookies, and we had more brandy as well. She talked; I listened.

"Well. The first thing you should know about Emma is that she was always a bit of a hellion. Do people still use that word? It sounds so old-fashioned now, but it describes her perfectly. A little crazy, I guess—and I mean that in the nicest way. She just seemed to have so much *energy*, more than any of the other women at Stanton.

"I first met her in the dormitory room to which we'd been assigned together. I'd just gotten off the plane, and I had two big suitcases with me. I was going to unpack and take a shower before going downstairs to register for classes. It was my first time in New York, and I didn't know anyone here. I was awfully tired from the trip, really, but I was soon to forget all about that fact! Suddenly, the door burst open and this tall, beautiful blond girl bounded into the room.

" 'Hello, hello,' she said. 'You're Jennifer from the Virgin Islands, I'm you're roommate Emma, I'm going to call you Jenny if that's all right with you because Jennifer is just too much of a mouthful, I love that suit you're wearing, come on, we're meeting some other freshmen I just met for a tour of the campus, then we're all going to register for the same classes, don't worry about those cases, I'll help you unpack later, come *on*, Jenny, the others are waiting!' That's how she used to speak, in one long run-on sentence. Then she was out the door again. I followed her, of course: what else could I do? She was always in charge of everything around her.

"So we took all the same classes. We were roommates in the dorm for our first two years, then we moved off campus for our junior and senior years. I wanted to rent a little place near campus, maybe try one of those women's hotels, but Emma was having none of that. She leased a two bedroom co-op on Madison and Sixty-fifth! I thought that was so exotic. She even hired a cleaning woman. I knew she was very rich, but even so . . . oh, well, we lived there until we graduated. Emma still lives there, with her husband.

"I wish I could convey to you the impression she made on me, Joe. Some people are just so full of life, you know? I understand her mother, Laura, was very much the same when she was young. Before life intervened."

"What does that mean?" I asked.

"Before she married Walter and had Emma and her sister: before she became a matron. The way Emma told it— when she spoke of her mother at all, which was very rare— it was all that pent-up energy, that suppressed *joie de vivre*, that probably led to her mother's tragedy. She named Emma after Madame Bovary, you know. It was her favorite story. Anyway, Emma hasn't changed a bit. But her husband, Stanley Smith—well, you'll meet him at the dinner party. I'll be very interested to know what you think of him.''

''What do *you* think of him, Jenny?''

She shrugged, and her eyebrows came together in concentration. ''Attractive, friendly, rather quiet—and rather sinister.''

''Sinister?''

''I don't want to elaborate,'' she said with finality. ''I only spoke to him for a few minutes at the reunion, and you know what they say about first impressions. Judge for yourself.''

I nodded and offered her a cookie. After a while I said, ''Why does Emma think someone's trying to kill her?''

Jenny sipped her coffee. ''Oh, I gather it's beyond the thinking stage. There have apparently been at least two attempts on her life. Someone tried to sideswipe her car a few weeks ago. And there was another incident involving a bottle of sleeping pills—she ended up in the Lenox Hill emergency room after that one. She didn't go into details; we weren't alone together for very long at the reunion. But she said she wanted to tell me all about it as soon as possible. I think I'd like you to be there when she does.'' She looked at me again, in that way she has, directly into my eyes.

''In that case,'' I said, ''I will.''

We talked a while longer, but it was mainly about other things. Old times, old acquaintances, our families, the major details of our lives between then and now. All the usual topics for two people meeting after years apart, despite the fact that there is nothing usual about our relationship. It was a little strained, I suppose, but not as difficult as I had expected. Perhaps, I thought, it was possible for us to become friends, after all.

After she left that night, I sat in front of my ersatz fire for a long time, remembering St. Thomas seven years ago. I remembered what had happened to me then, and the crucial role Jenny Hughes had played in it. Now, all these years later, she had come to me for help, and I knew I would do anything I possibly could do for her.

As I've said, Jenny once saved my life. I won't elaborate on it now: I've recorded the whole story elsewhere. But on that rainy night in February, I was thinking of that time, of the strange series of events that had bonded the two of us to each other in a way that no two people should ever be bonded. It's unnatural, really, but there it was. I was—am—beholden to her. I had a deep feeling of guilt, and a debt to pay. I would try to help Jenny's friend because, in doing so, I would be helping Jenny herself.

That was how I became involved in all this.

My first encounter with violent death, seven years ago, forever altered the direction of my life. This, my second experience of it, set me on a new course.

TWO

The Princess of Pure Delight

Fifth Avenue isn't merely an address in New York. In a way, the section of the avenue that faces Central Park is a symbol of a certain way of life that is alien to most people, despite the fact that it still exists. The sidewalks that line the avenue are very wide and sparkling clean. The canopies that mark the entrances to the big apartment buildings are quietly, tastefully decorated with the building's number, and the smart uniforms of the doormen usually match the color of the canopy.

Beyond the glass doors can be glimpsed lobbies; marbled, carpeted masterpieces of muted lighting, and plush couches and chairs of muted design and color on which no one is ever to be found sitting. In fact, these beautifully appointed lobbies are forever empty. They are simply a pleasant passage to the paneled elevators with their silent, smiling operators in uniforms that match those on the doormen, who take the tenants quietly and quickly upward to the private foyers outside palatial apartments with balconies overlooking the park.

Some of the residents in these dramatic quarters will be found listed in the so-called blue book, but most of them are far too well-bred to announce themselves in so crass a way. The blue book was always frowned upon by the true Old Money, and simply being listed there automatically relegated you to the Second String. There are as many tiers of society here as elsewhere, with one major difference: everyone is rich. This makes class distinction far less visible, but no less real.

Bradley Masterson, Emma's great-grandfather, would have welcomed his family's inclusion in the legendary blue book. He was a self-made man, and he didn't care who knew it. In fact, the more who knew, the better, as far as he was concerned. The Mastersons and the Vales, for all their power in the business world, were definitely New Money.

And how does Joseph Wilder, novelist and playwright, in his postage-stamp West Village digs, know so much about this part of town? Well, it's my part of town, too. I grew up in St. Thomas, but my mother grew up not four blocks from Sarah Masterson's apartment. So did her parents, and their parents, right on back to some stately home of England and several kings and queens who were my ancestors. My mom, Linda, now lives here again, two blocks and ten street numbers south of Sarah Masterson. Small world.

To Jenny's surprise, it was about to get much smaller.

"Joe Wilder!" Sarah Masterson cried as she glided toward us across her marble foyer. "How lovely to see you! I was delighted when I learned that you were going to be here."

Jenny stared. She had told me, on the way here, that after the initial informal invitation from Emma at the reunion, she had received a note from Sarah Masterson repeating the offer. Jenny had sent a note back on her own stationery, naming me as her escort. That's how invitations are extended and accepted in this part of town—and that's how Mrs. Masterson had learned of my inclusion at the dinner party. But, judging from her expression, Jenny was amazed to learn the little secret I had deliberately kept from her.

I smiled. "Hello, Mrs. Masterson. It's been a while."

"It certainly has. I haven't seen you at the ballet with your mother in quite some time. How is Linda?"

"She's fine. I told her I'd be here tonight, and she said to tell you she'd see you in a couple of weeks."

"Ah, yes, *Swan Lake*," Mrs. Masterson said, nodding. Then she turned and embraced the woman at my side. "Jenny, darling, welcome back to New York!"

"Thank you, Mrs. Masterson. You're looking well."

"And so are you. I think you know most of the people here, so you can introduce Joe around. We're very informal tonight, and *guess* who isn't here yet!"

The two of them laughed as a smiling young woman in a maid's uniform took our coats.

"I'm not a bit surprised," Jenny said. "Emma has always loved being the last to arrive: that way she gets to make an entrance."

Sarah Masterson nodded, and a sad smile flashed briefly on her face. "Yes. Her mother was like that, too." Then the sadness disappeared as she led us into the living room. "Come meet everyone."

If the room had been smaller, the five people in it would have seemed a sizable crowd. As it was, they barely made a dent in it. Thirty by twenty, I would imagine, with creamy white furniture and carpets. Glass-topped coffee table; lots of glass and chrome shelves lining the walls with dramatically lit figurines; several large paintings—including the Warhol portrait of Laura Vale—on the white walls; an impressively big, state-of-the-art home entertainment center; a shiny white grand piano. Glass doors led out to the flower-lined terrace, beyond which the Manhattan skyline winked and glistened. This was New York as only glimpsed in magazines and Cole Porter musicals. I *really* should think about moving, I thought, as Jenny and I stood smiling around at everyone.

They smiled back. Three men and two women, beautifully dressed, the men in dark suits and the women in bright dresses. Two young couples and a distinguished looking, silver-haired older man. Everybody had nice hair and beautiful teeth, and the men's ties, like mine, were Countess Mara—some rules of Upper East Side fashion come and go, but others remain forever. Your basic rich WASP dinner party, I decided.

Mistake number one. One of the young women, the tall brunette in the flower-print dress, immediately jumped up from a couch and ran into Jenny's arms.

"Hello again, sweetie," she said before turning to me. "Hi, I'm Rachel Cohen—Jenny and Emma and I went to Stanton together. That's my husband, Dave Cohen. You're Joseph Wilder, and I'm a fan of yours."

I smiled. "Please call me Joe." Her husband, a slight man with curly brown hair and a pleasant demeanor, rose to shake my hand as I amended my impression of the group: not so WASP-y, after all, what with Jenny and the Cohens. Good.

I turned to the others. The old man was introduced to me as Daniel Gillespie, the family attorney and one of Sarah Masterson's oldest friends. WASP City: from the Upper East Side firm of Gillespie, Gillespie, and Gillespie, no doubt, by way of Newport, Palm Beach, and Darien, where most of his clients probably lived. He reminded me of my older male relatives. He smiled, nearly crushing my hand in his surprising grip. The pretty, rather plump, dark-haired young woman seated on the other couch would probably be—

"Sarah Vale," she whispered, smiling as she reached up to shake my hand.

I smiled down at Sarah Masterson's younger grand-daughter, Emma's sister. She would be about—I did the math in my head—twenty-eight, and she had a broad face and dark eyes. Attractive, certainly, but no beauty. I thought of the pictures I'd seen of her mother, Laura, and Jenny's description of her blond, blue-eyed sister.

"Hello, Sarah," Jenny said. "It's been a while."

"Yes," Emma's sister said. "Let's see, ten years. I'd just finished my freshman year at Stanton when you and Emma and Rachel graduated. And you'll recognize my date tonight, as well." She pointed over toward the dark corner just in front of the picture windows.

A very tall man in a black suit was standing in the shadows there, and as we looked over at him he stepped forward, grinning, into the light of the crystal chandelier. I heard Jenny emit a small gasp, as well she might. He was six-four, at least, powerfully built, with brown eyes and wavy, almost blue-black hair. He looked like nothing so much as the young Rock Hudson.

"Jenny Hughes!" the man said, coming up to greet her.

"Craig! Hello. How—how nice to see you. I, um—"

Whatever Jenny was about to say—or, rather, stammer—died on her lips as the front door buzzer sounded. She quickly turned to me, covering her gaffe. "Joe, this is Craig Davis. Craig, Joseph Wilder."

I was shaking hands with Craig Davis when it happened. Our hostess came back into the room arm in arm with a woman who could only be Emma Masterson Vale. Everyone turned in her direction, and the room was suddenly quiet. One moment we were all standing around saying howdy, and in the next moment this force of nature was upon us.

She was blond, and she was wearing a white dress, and I remember thinking that her mother's portrait on the wall behind me had somehow come to life. But her physical appearance, lovely as it was, was secondary. It is the energy that I remember now, the energy that suddenly seemed to be filling the room. I stared as she came over to embrace Jenny and meet me, thinking briefly of someone else, a young woman in St. Thomas seven years ago. Then I smiled and introduced myself.

"Hello, Joe," she said. "I'm Emma, and this"—she

waved, indicating the man who stood just behind her, whose presence I hadn't even noticed—"is my husband, Stanley. Oh, Jenny, am I glad to see *you*! Old home week. How's your new apartment?"

"It's getting there," Jenny said. "As soon as everything's in place, I'll have you over so you can see for yourself."

"I'll hold you to that. In the meantime, welcome back to New York. We have a tradition here you may remember called Sunday brunch. Are you available day after tomorrow? Just the two of us, of course. . . ."

Jenny glanced at me. I read her silent question and nodded.

"Tell you what, Em, let's make it just the *three* of us. I—I think Joe may be able to—to—"

Jenny trailed off, and the bright smile left her friend's face.

"Oh," Emma said. "Oh, I see." The smile immediately came back into place, and she turned it on me. "Okay, the three of us, then. My place, Sunday, noon." She squeezed Jenny's hand and took off, a lovely blur of blond hair and white dress and flashing teeth, into Rachel Cohen's waiting arms. "Hello there! Gosh, you look gorgeous tonight!"

"So do you, sweetie. . . ."

I tore my gaze from Emma Vale Smith and turned to the man who was still standing uncertainly beside us. Stanley Smith was attractive, as Jenny had said. About my height—six-one—and weight, with sandy hair and a nice tan. In February. Either he'd been on vacation recently or his health club had a UV-A facility. The latter, I decided. He wore a nice blue suit, and something instinctively told me that Emma had bought it for him, and the shirt and Countess Mara tie to go with it, not to mention the health club membership.

It was his eyes. Good-looking, well-dressed, polite—but not sinister. That was the word Jenny had used to describe him. I could see why she'd used it, but she was wrong. It was the expression in his eyes that had given her the impression, the way he looked at everything. He gazed around the room—people, furnishings, objects—in a certain way I've noticed before. Hungrily, as if he were drinking it all in, savoring it. Jenny would have noticed this at the Waldorf, but she'd misinterpreted it. He was simply not accustomed to being in such rooms, with such people. His wife had opened the door.

I could practically feel his discomfort. I smiled at him. "So, I'm a writer, novels and plays. What's your line, Mr. Smith?"

"Stan," he corrected with a nervous smile. "I'm a broker, with Adams and Sterling."

"Private portfolios?" I ventured.

"Among other things, yes."

"Well, then," I said, "let's talk after dinner."

He grinned, visibly relaxing. "Sure! Excuse me." He left us and went to join his wife with her grandmother.

Jenny was watching me. "Thinking of investing, Joe?"

I smiled, leaning over to whisper. "As a matter of fact, yes. But you're wrong about him. Later."

She nodded, and we actually shared a little laugh. We were developing a private shorthand.

Craig Davis came back over to us.

"So, Jenny," he said, "I understand you've moved to New York. How could you bear to leave St. Thomas for this, especially in the winter?"

Jenny shrugged, smiling. "It was time for a change. There was nothing keeping me there, lovely as it is. I quit my job recently, and I'm looking into new possibilities. What—um—what are you up to these days?"

He shrugged, grinning. "Oh, you know, same old same old. I'm living with Sarah now."

"Oh," Jenny said evenly. "How nice."

He grinned again and drifted off to join another group. I watched him go, wondering what my life would be like if I were that gorgeous. Then I turned to Jenny.

" 'Same old same old'?" I asked. "What, exactly, does he do?"

She shook her head in grim amusement. "A little acting, a little modeling, a little bartending. . . ."

"I see," I said, giving her my sage Joe Wilder nod. "Idle rich boy."

She laughed. "Idle *poor* boy is closer to the truth. His family cut him off without a cent—after he used up his trust fund, of course."

"Why?"

"Because he doesn't *do* anything. He never *learned* to do anything. Decorative, as opposed to functional. He's big and beautiful and completely useless."

"Ouch!" I murmured. "I gather he's not your favorite person. You were surprised to see him here with Sarah tonight. Is he an old lover of yours?"

Jenny stared at the handsome man across the room, slowly shaking her head.

"No," she whispered at last. "Emma's."

"Oh." I followed her gaze to Craig Davis, then over to Sarah Vale. Then I turned and looked at Emma Vale Smith. "Oh."

"Yeah," Jenny said. "Oh."

I thought about that as everyone milled about for the next twenty minutes or so, chatting pleasantly, until Sarah Masterson led us into the dining room.

The rest of the party—dinner and dessert, then coffee and cordials in the living room—was a cavalcade of impressions, a series of tableaux that I would recall in the following days. As it turned out, it was fortunate that I remembered everything so clearly.

I was seated to the right of the hostess at the long table in the dining room. Her granddaughter, Sarah, was on my other side, and Stan Smith was directly across from me. Mr. Gillespie played host at the other end of the table, flanked by Emma and Jenny. Jenny was just in my line of vision, with a floral centerpiece and an ornate silver candelabrum between us, but now and then I shifted slightly in my seat and caught her gaze. She was watching me watching them.

While keeping up my end of conversations with both Sarahs, I managed to notice several things. The young Sarah kept casting nervous glances across at Craig Davis, who was between Jenny and Rachel Cohen. He was openly flirting with Rachel, who flirted right back with innocent good nature. His actions seemed mundane enough, but they certainly made his lover jittery. The obvious conclusion was that Sarah didn't feel very secure in the relationship. Looking at the plump, rather plain girl beside me, then over at the matinee idol, I couldn't say I blamed her for being nervous.

I dismissed the Cohens and Mr. Gillespie, insofar as my present mission—to observe possible suspects—was concerned. Of course, I had yet to hear the details of the alleged attempts on Emma Vale Smith's life, but even then I realized that Emma's girlfriend and her husband were as unlikely as the family solicitor to wish to harm someone from whose death they would not profit.

By the time dessert was served, I liked Stanley Smith just fine. There was something endearing about his gaucherie. Several times, when new courses were lowered before us, I saw him surreptitiously watching Mrs. Masterson and me, making sure that he picked up the same fork as everyone else. At one point he noticed that his wineglass was empty. He picked it up, glancing behind him to see if any of the people serving us was nearby. Finding no one there at the moment, he turned toward Mrs. Masterson. I could see him forming the obvious question on his lips, so I leaned forward and spoke to him, asking him if he was a fan of any New York sports teams. As I spoke, I indicated with my hand that he should put the glass down. He did so at once, nodding his thanks. Moments later, someone arrived to refill the empty glasses, and Stanley, Mrs. Masterson, and I had a lively discussion about the Yankees.

Of course, I reminded myself, Stan was Emma's husband, and he presumably had the most to gain from her
sudden demise. Then I dismissed the thought and made an
effort to concentrate on the festivities.

That concentration was constantly interrupted. Back in
the living room, sipping coffee from a tiny cup, I noticed
some other things. Emma was almost always the center of
attention, and twice she said things that made the whole
room laugh. Well, everyone but her sister, who sat across
the room, clutching Craig's arm. In fact, throughout the
entire evening, the two sisters did not exchange a single
word. Furthermore, I soon discovered that, other than saying hello and goodbye, Emma and Craig Davis did not
speak to each other. She barely even looked in his direction,
but now and then I noticed that he was watching her rather
intently. Interesting.

Stan and I went out onto the terrace for our financial
discussion. We smoked cigarettes in the cold, looking out
at the darkness of Central Park and the millions of lights
surrounding it, and he gave me a brief dissertation on how
he managed personal portfolios. He seemed nice enough,
and he obviously knew what he was talking about. I told
him that I might be interested in his services, which was
perfectly true, and he handed me an engraved business card
before we went back inside.

The party ended shortly after that, and Jenny and I were
the first to leave. We thanked our hostess, said good-bye
to everyone else, and were silently ushered down in the
elevator. We waited in the marbled lobby while the liveried
doorman hailed us a cab, and then we were off down Fifth
Avenue.

''Why didn't you tell me you and Mrs. Masterson knew
each other?''

I could tell from the tone of Jenny's voice that she'd
been waiting all evening to ask me that, and the cab had

barely pulled away from the curb before she blurted it out.

"We don't know each other, really," I said, settling back in the plush leather seat. "She and my mom have adjoining seats at the Met. American Ballet Theater. They met there a few years ago, and they got to talking during intermission. Their seats are in the first row of the orchestra, practically on the stage. Unfashionably close, they both admitted, but they love it so much they don't care. When they recognized in each other a fellow fanatic, they began calling each other at the beginning of every season, to make sure they'd attend the same performances. They each get two tickets to everything on offer, and Mom used to drag me to a few of them—until she realized she'd never convert me. All those sylphs and swans just give me the willies." I paused, glancing over at her. No reaction. I tried it again. "I said, all those sylphs and swans—"

"Yes," she interjected, smiling. "I got it. 'The willies.' Very funny."

"Thank you. It's my *only* ballet joke, I promise. But that's how I met Mrs. Masterson. We even had dinner with her once, at that restaurant in the Met. But I haven't been to the ballet in a long time. She and my mother both have girlfriends who usually go with them. So I wouldn't actually say I *know* her very well. She's an acquaintance."

Jenny nodded, and for a while we rode in silence. I was still getting used to being with her, with this woman I hadn't seen in seven years. I was glad, sitting there beside her in the cab, to realize that I was beginning to feel a lot more comfortable with her.

"So, what do you think?" she asked me as we approached Gramercy Park.

I smiled over at her. "I think it was a nice party. Thank you for inviting me."

She rolled her eyes. "You're welcome. Now, what do you think of Emma?"

"She's lovely," I said.

"And the others?"

‎ ''They're lovely, too.''

‎ ''Yes, but could any of them be trying to—you know. . . .''

I smiled at her again. ''Well, I think Mrs. Peacock is in the clear, but Colonel Mustard is definitely on my list of suspects.''

''Oh, you!'' she said. Then, in spite of her exasperation, she laughed. Good, I thought: she's beginning to feel more comfortable, too.

''I think I'll reserve all judgment until Sunday,'' I told her. ''I want to hear what Emma has to tell us.''

As the cab slowed to make the turn into her street, she said, ''Yes. Yes, I suppose that would be best . . .''

THREE

O Fabulous One

"No," Emma Vale Smith replied, "I haven't been to the police."

This was the obvious answer to my obvious question the following Sunday morning, in Emma's pretty apartment on Madison and Sixty-fifth. Unlike her grandmother on Fifth Avenue, she did not have two separate rooms for entertaining and dining, merely two halves of a large, L-shaped area. The kitchen—replete with all the latest models of Masterson appliances—was visible through a doorway and a pass-through on one side of the dining area, and a hallway led away from the living room area to the two bedrooms and bath.

We had dined on eggs, bacon, and cinnamon toast that Emma had apparently prepared on her Masterson range and in her Masterson toaster oven herself: there was no one else there, just the three of us. Stan had gone to the gym, she told us, and the housekeeper didn't come in on weekends.

Now we were in the living area, drinking coffee. Emma, in pink hostess pajamas, was on the big white couch beside Jenny. I was in an amazingly comfortable reclining armchair, facing them across the coffee table. I noticed that her

television, VCR, and music system were all Mastersons.
The two longer walls were covered with floor-to-ceiling
bookshelves, and all the shelves were full. The other walls
and the furniture were various shades of white and beige,
prompting me to wonder if she and her grandmother had
the same decorator. I wouldn't have been a bit surprised.

At that time, I had not really formed a clear impression
of her. I wasn't even certain whether or not I liked her. She
was lovely, she was energetic, she was rich, and she was
one of Jenny's closest friends. But, other than those basic
facts, I had yet to get a distinct feel for her. I am constantly
reminding myself not to jump to conclusions, as I frequently do, and I remember doing it that morning in her
apartment. I would wait and see.

By previous agreement, Jenny and I had kept the talk small
while we brunched. Actually, I kept it *very* small, not saying much of anything as the two women caught up on each
other's lives, with liberal sprinklings of irrelevant and
somewhat salacious gossip about former classmates and acquaintances. I gathered that Emma was familiar with the
events in St. Thomas seven years ago: she and Jenny had
been in frequent contact with each other ever since college.

I also got a thumbnail history of Emma's life from college to the present. There were a lot of giggling references
to her "wild years," which apparently spanned the time
from graduation to about five years ago, when she would
have been about twenty-six. Sex, drugs, rock and roll. Several seasons on the Continent with her Continental counterparts: Eurotrash, as they're now called. The Greek
islands, Swiss ski resorts, movie stars' children, a Chelsea
flat with two soon-to-be-world-famous models. Several affairs, one with an Academy Award–winning British actor.
He left her for a teenaged starlet, I was not surprised to
learn, and Emma enjoyed two weeks on the front pages
of every cheesy tabloid in the world ("Oscar Winner
Pulls Plug On Electronics Heiress!—Refrigerator Girl

Burned!''). The usual stuff—well, *usual* for the great-granddaughter of Bradley Masterson, at any rate.

She'd managed to have a great deal of fun, and to avoid trouble. *Serious* trouble, she amended, laughing: there *was* that business about the restaurant in Cairo that practically burned to the ground when her date and another man, the nephew of a sheikh, decided to stage a swordfight with their flaming shish kebabs. The two men spent several hours in jail, laughing hysterically, before Emma was able to bail them out, apparently with a platinum bracelet. And a jolly time was had by all.

About five years ago, Emma had suddenly grown tired of her travels and her companions and her everybody-into-the-pool lifestyle. She returned to New York, to her bemused grandmother and her furious father. Walter Vale and his second wife had been scandalized by her headline-making shenanigans, although there was little they could do to stop her: her trust fund, arranged by her mother, was ironclad. Emma didn't give a damn what her father and stepmother thought of her, as she'd had little to do with them all her adult life. Her grandmother, whom she adored, had looked stern and told her to behave. Then Sarah Masterson had smiled and taken Emma, the light of her life, into her arms.

And that's how you punish a trust fund baby.

The last five years had been infinitely more stable. Emma had actually gone to work at Masterson Electronics, in the promotion department, where she and two assistants were responsible for overseeing the Madison Avenue advertising agency that handled them. She'd also taken to sitting in on the corporation's monthly board meetings and annual shareholders' meetings—again thanks to Laura and her great-grandfather, she held more shares than any other single person, including President Walter. In addition to all this, she helped her grandmother with several social activities, including—surprise!—American Ballet Theater.

And she'd married Stanley Smith, a little more than one year ago.

Shortly after Emma returned to New York, her old lover from her college days, Craig Davis, had briefly reentered her life. Her father and stepmother, among other people, had entertained great hopes for a match. Craig was the middle son (and black sheep) of *the* Davis family, of car dealership fame. It was thought by everyone—including Craig—that marrying Emma Masterson Vale and settling down would place him back in the bosom of his family. Alas, this was not to be: Emma threw him over for a second time, and for the first reason all over again.

Craig, for all his beauty, was apparently a vapid, shiftless Adonis type who'd never had a steady job. He'd squandered the *de rigeur* trust fund on parties and round-the-world adventures, fast cars, fast women, major booze, minor drugs, and all the rest of it. I remembered Jenny's words from the dinner party, that he'd never learned to do anything. Emma hadn't liked that during their first affair, and she certainly didn't need it now, after she'd had so many similarly useless lovers all over America and Europe and points east.

But the *real* reason Emma had broken up with Craig this time, she now confided, was that her father and her stepmother actually *approved* of him. I was beginning to realize that Emma hated her father, and that the feeling was apparently mutual. I couldn't *wait* to meet Walter Vale . . .

So, Craig had transferred his attention to Emma's younger sister, and about a year and a half ago, Emma had met a nice, bright, nervous young stockbroker in an East Village dance club. Stanley Smith had asked her to dance, and later he'd driven her home. He called her the next day, asking her to dinner. She went. She learned that he lived in Brooklyn, and that he'd been born and raised there. He'd worked his way through NYU, with the help of a scholarship. He'd gotten a job at Adams and Sterling by the most astonishing of means: he'd actually impressed the partner who reluctantly interviewed him with his résumé and his sensible ideas. He'd worked his way up from glorified gofer to portfolio management in a mere three years—and he was the only one there who couldn't trace his family back to Magna Carta.

Emma had fallen in love with him.

Her father had not.

That clinched it, as far as Emma was concerned. They'd been married in a registry office in City Hall, with Stan's brother and Emma's friend Rachel Cohen as witnesses and her grandmother and Mr. Gillespie the only invited guests, and Stan had moved from his family home in Brooklyn to this apartment. He and Emma had been happy for a whole year.

Their year of happiness had been capped with what is commonly referred to as a blessed event. Emma turned to Jenny at this point, took Jenny's hands in hers, and announced to the two of us that she was pregnant. She and Stan had learned of it two months ago, just before Christmas, and they had announced it only to family and friends. I watched the two friends embrace, glancing automatically at Emma's stomach. There was a slight swelling there, I supposed, never having seen her before, but she wasn't really showing yet. At any rate, the happy marriage had become a *very* happy one.

Until five weeks ago, when, Emma said, her car had been sideswiped on the FDR Drive, and she had narrowly missed a fatal crash. Then, about three weeks ago, she had taken a sleeping capsule from the prescription bottle in her medicine cabinet. The capsule had contained aspirin, to which she was fatally allergic, rather than the usual medication. Twenty minutes later she was in the emergency room.

Which brought us to the living room, and our present conversation.

"Why not?" Jenny asked. "Why not just report it to the police?"

Emma sighed and raised her eyebrows. "And say what, exactly? That I had some difficulty with my car? That I mistakenly took aspirin instead of a sleeping pill? The police were involved briefly when I arrived at the hospital, but that's standard procedure, and they didn't believe me, anyway. I'm that kooky heiress, remember? I think I'd have a little problem with credibility."

"Do you?" I asked as evenly as possible.

She looked over at me. "Do I what?"

"Have a problem with credibility?"

Emma sighed again. "I'm not crazy, Joe, and my party days are behind me. Five weeks ago I was on my way to my weekly appointment with my chiropractor in the Village. One minute I was sailing down the FDR, and the next thing I knew, some big black car was ramming me from behind. Then it got next to me and tried to force me into the fast lane, into another car. I remember looking over at the tinted windows: I couldn't see a thing, just the glint of the sunlight. I managed to get over to the side and turn off the Drive, and by the time I stopped and looked back, the black car was long gone. I thought maybe it was a drunk driver, or something, and, to tell you the truth, I forgot about it. Then, two weeks later, after that awful party, I took a sleeping capsule and went into whatchamacallit shock . . ."

"Anaphylactic," Jenny supplied.

"Wait a minute," I interjected. "What awful party?"

"Oh, this anniversary thing. It was Stan's idea, actually, to have a first anniversary party and invite everyone we didn't ask to the wedding at City Hall. And to tell them all about the baby. Stan's family, my family, his colleagues at the brokerage, various higher-ups at Masterson—you know, like that. Everyone came, believe it or not, bearing gifts. The Smiths were very nice, considering that the Vale contingent fairly ignored them all evening. My father and stepmother were one step away from rude, and my sister and Craig made it clear that Stan's family was just too *Brooklyn* for them. Thank God for Grammy. She was lovely to everyone—well, except Dad, of course, but the two of them have never gotten along, especially since Mother's death and his remarriage.''

''All these people were here?'' I asked, waving my arm. ''In this apartment?''

''Yes. Thirty-two people, to be exact. Cocktails, a catered buffet, the inevitable champagne toast—Stan's father did that, because Dad and Ann were gone by then.''

''Ann?''

''My stepmother. Anyway, the last people finally left at about midnight. I helped the caterers clean up and got ready for bed. I don't often take a sleeping pill—and I know I shouldn't do it in my condition—but I was so wired from smiling at everyone . . . well, that's when it happened. Stan took me to Lenox Hill, and they put me on a respirator and gave me some whatever-you-call-it—''

''Antitoxin,'' Jenny said.

''—yeah, and I spent the night there. I was frantic about the baby, but they assured me that everything was all right. By the time the bottle was examined, there were only regular sleeping pills in it. There was a bottle of aspirin capsules beside it in the cabinet, for Stan, and they're red and white, just like my prescription. The police and the doctors decided I must have mixed them up. Even Stan thinks so. He hasn't said anything, but I know that's what he believes. I didn't tell him about the car, you see: you're the first people I've told about that. So, everybody thinks flaky Emma mixed up the bottles. Just one problem with that theory.''

I leaned forward. ''What?''

She looked straight into my eyes.

''I *didn't* mix them up,'' she said. ''Somebody tried to kill me. Like with the car. They've tried it twice now.''

She paused a moment, and I heard the sigh again, the little expulsion of air through her teeth that was apparently an unconscious mannerism. She was still looking at me. She wet her lips with her tongue and continued. "Listen, Joe, Jenny's mentioned you many times over the years. I—I know all about St. Thomas, and what you ... well, I was just wondering if maybe you could ..." She trailed off uncertainly, glancing over at Jenny and back to me. Then she took a deep breath and said, "I don't want anything to happen to my baby. I don't want to die."

We were all silent for a while, thinking about that. Jenny reached over to grasp her former roommate's hand. I watched them for a moment, arranging questions in my mind. The first one was easy.

"Are you sure you don't want a professional investigator looking into this?"

Emma shook her head, and her loose blond hair glistened. "No. Absolutely not. I mean, I'll pay you if—"

I raised my hand. "I'm not a professional. I can't even guarantee that I'll find out anything useful to you. The only other time I've ever"—I glanced briefly over at Jenny—"done anything like this, I was personally involved. I mean, I had a personal motive for finding out what was going on. But you're Jenny's friend, and that's good enough for me. I'll help you in any way I can. But remember: if I ever decide that the police should become involved, you're going to have to respect that. I understand your aversion to them, because my family is not unlike yours. You and I were brought up with some of the same rules. Police mean publicity, and publicity is to be avoided at all times, at all costs, right?"

She surprised me by bursting into laughter. She threw her head back, fairly whooping with humor. When she calmed down a little, she said, "The Masterson credo, right on the nose! I've already broken it a few times, what with movie stars and Egyptian prisons and God knows what other nonsense!'' Then her laughter stopped, and she was once again serious. ''It's strange, but now, when I look back at some of the things I've done, it all seems to have happened to some other woman. I'm not that girl now. I'm a responsible, productive, married woman. I'm expecting a child, of all things! Who would ever have predicted it? At the rate I was going, I'm sometimes amazed that I'm still here at all! I like myself now—better than I ever liked the old model.''

I smiled, remembering Jenny's tale of Emma's unwavering loyalty toward the minority students at Stanton College. ''Oh, don't dismiss the old model so easily. She didn't sound so terrible. From what I've heard, I'd say you've always been a nice person.''

I had surprised myself by saying that. I was supposed to be keeping an open mind, and yet I couldn't help warming to her. There was something about her . . .

Emma glanced over at the woman beside her, squeezing the hand she still held. ''Yes. Jenny. And Rachel. If we're judged by our friends, I guess I'm not so bad, at that!''

She and Jenny smiled at each other, then turned their grins on me. They hadn't planned the effect, of course, but it was there just the same. In that moment, I knew that I would do anything for them. I took a deep breath and began the interrogation.

''Okay,'' I said, settling back in the comfortable armchair as Jenny leaned forward to pour us all more coffee. ''First question: may I smoke?''

The three of us laughed, and some slight tension I'd been feeling in the room seemed to dissipate. Good.

Emma pushed a big crystal ashtray across the coffee table toward me. ''If I can't stop my husband, I'm certainly not going to stop you. Just blow the smoke the other way, please: I'm breathing for two now.''

I nodded and lit up. ''Second question, and please think

before you answer this. Do you have any idea who might wish to harm you?"

She didn't have to think: she'd obviously already thought. She shook her head immediately. "No, none. I mean, what sort of enemies could I have? I know I'm the principal shareholder in Masterson Electronics, but I don't interfere with the actual running of the place. Not that I could: I don't really know that much about it. I majored in English, like my mother." She waved toward the floor-to ceiling bookshelves. "But I minored in graphic and commercial art, which vaguely qualifies me for the position I've taken at Masterson. My two assistants are ambitious, but they're not *murderously* ambitious, so I think we can write them off. My friends—well, Jenny and Rachel are probably my closest friends, and the others are perfectly nice people, too." She shrugged. "Enemies. Gosh, I just can't think of any."

Smooth, I thought. She'd carefully avoided the obvious. I would have to introduce the subject myself.

"What about your family?" I asked.

Emma Vale Smith's lovely blue eyes widened in what I could only interpret as genuine astonishment. She looked over at Jenny, as if for some help or support, but Jenny was displaying a sudden, intense interest in the surface of the coffee table before her. The surprised blue stare swept back toward me.

"My *family*?!" she cried. "Stan? Grammy? You think *they'd* want to hurt me? That's insane!"

No it isn't, I thought. Sarah Masterson was not a suspect, as far as I could see, but Emma's husband was a different matter entirely. I let it slide.

"What about the *rest* of your family?" I suggested, surprised at how quiet my own voice sounded.

No fireworks this time. Emma merely shrugged her shoulders. When she spoke, her voice was subdued, not unlike my own.

"You'd have to ask them," she murmured.

There was a long moment of silence after that. I leaned forward to crush out my cigarette, looking over at Jenny as I did so. She had been sitting quietly throughout our conversation, contributing nothing, but I could tell from the look of concern she now gave her friend that she hadn't missed a single thing. I wondered what she was thinking. I turned my attention back to our hostess.

"Tell me about Sarah," I finally said.

Emma looked puzzled. "Grammy?"

"No, I mean your sister, Sarah Vale."

"Oh. *Her.*" Emma shrugged again, and this time she augmented the action with a bemused shake of her head. "Two women: one name. And they couldn't be more different if they tried." She sighed again, settling back into the couch. "*Sarah* isn't trying to kill me."

I raised my eyebrows, noting the slight emphasis she used every time she uttered her sister's name. It was apparently unconscious.

"How can you be so sure of that?" I asked her.

The intense blue gaze was once again leveled at me. "Joe, have you ever heard me curse?"

"No."

"Well, brace yourself. *Sarah* isn't trying to kill me because *Sarah* is an asshole."

Long pause.

"Oh," I said.

Then we were all laughing. Emma fell back against the couch, clutching her stomach as she screamed. I looked at Jenny, who nodded to me as she giggled: she shared Emma's opinion of her sister. I was laughing at the sight of them, and at the laughter itself, this oldest friends/girls together/sorority house thing that was going on between them. They caught each other's eye, which merely set them both off again. This had happened before, many times.

When we regained our composure, I said, "You don't think Sarah is capable of these attempts?"

"Oh, I suppose she's *capable*," Emma admitted. "I just don't think she'd *do* it. She's so white-bread, you know?"

"White-bread?"

"Beige, blah, namby-pamby. All of the above. Choose one. In twenty-eight years, I don't think she's ever misbehaved. I wouldn't be surprised to learn that she's still a virgin." She thought of something, and her eyebrows came together. "Well, yes I would . . ."

"Ah," I said, leaning forward. "Craig Davis."

Emma nodded. "Yeah. The beautiful Craig. He'd hang around a virgin for exactly three seconds before he changed her mind or got out of town. But what he's doing with *her*, I just can't fathom." Another unconscious sigh and a shrug. "Oh, well, she's paying the rent."

"And where is she doing that?" I asked her.

"Over on the west side. She's had a place there since she graduated. Eighty-first and West End."

I was reaching in my jacket for a pen when I happened to glance over at Jenny. Smiling, I lowered my hand. She had already produced a pen and notepad from her purse, and she was ready for action.

"What's the address?" she asked Emma.

Emma told her. Jenny wrote it down, throwing a brief smile over at me as she did so. I smiled back, thinking, Della Street lives. Then I returned my attention to Emma.

"Why didn't you tell your husband about the incident on the FDR Drive?"

Some women look incredibly pretty when they blush. Emma Vale Smith was one of them.

"I didn't tell him," she said, "because I'm his wife. I'm about to bear his child. I'm trying to make a home here with a man I happen to love very much."

She stood up from the couch and wandered over to the picture window along the far wall. She stopped there, her back to us, gazing out at Madison Avenue as she continued.

"From the night we met, at that club in the Village, I've been making a conscious effort to—to present myself to him a certain way. To *be* the real me. Not that crazy rich girl who knocked around all over the world, doing nothing in particular, contributing nothing. Looking for love, as the song says, in all the wrong places, simply because, with the exception of Grammy, there is no love for me in my family. Even now, after a whole year of marriage, I start every day by wondering, is this it? Is today the day he looks at me and sees a spoiled, self-serving, rich bitch? I don't *ever* want him to meet her."

She turned back to us then. A single tear moved slowly down her cheek, and the sun came through the window behind her, playing in her hair. "And the *last* thing I want him to know is that someone might be trying to kill me for my money."

Jenny and I watched her as she came back across the room and resumed her place on the couch.

"I think you may be underestimating him," I told her, hoping that it was the truth.

She smiled sadly and shook her head, and I heard the sigh again. "I'd rather not test that theory, just the same. If there's one thing I've learned about men, it's that they have this ingrained need to be perceived as the providers, even when they're not. It's a sociological thing, I guess, as old as time. The man doesn't like being constantly reminded that the woman he's supposed to be providing for is a hell of a lot richer than he'll ever be."

I nodded, wondering which man had taught her that lesson. Craig Davis? The British movie star? Not that it mattered: I'm a man, and I knew she was right. The best of us are feminists—until it comes to *that*.

So. Now I knew that she was bright, and perceptive, and very worried. I was beginning to form an opinion of her, and it was a good one.

Finally, I asked her the sixty-four-thousand-dollar question.

"Emma," I said, speaking slowly as I watched her, "do you have a will?"

FOUR

Paradise in the Hold

Monday morning dawned bright and fair. Well, as bright and fair as weather in the low forties can be, but at least the sky was relatively clear. The sun was actually shining, which isn't bad for New York in late February.

I use *dawned* in the poetic sense, you understand. I grew up in a house with my mother, an actress, director, and producer, and she's always kept theater hours. I majored in drama when I came to New York from the Virgin Islands for college, and when I moved to the city I was an actor for a while before I sat down and wrote my first play. I've written six plays now, in addition to four published novels, and four of the plays have been produced, three of them off-Broadway. One of them was even videotaped and shown on PBS, in the *Theater in America* series. It was called *Me Again*, and it starred Scott Bakula and Mare Winningham. My only comedy, so far. But enough of all that: the point is that I keep theater hours, too. I write late into the night, and I get up closer to noon than dawn.

Ask a writer for the time and he'll give you his résumé.

So, the time was about eleven-thirty Monday morning. I was meeting Emma at two o'clock, so I woke up Mr. Coffee and phoned Jenny. She'd been up for hours, apparently, and I could hear loud thumps and male voices in the background.

"My new couch just arrived," Jenny informed me over the din. "Hang on a moment, Joe—no, not there, *there*, yes, thank you—Joe? Sorry, I'm directing traffic here. Is there something specific you wanted, because—"

I can be quick-witted, even in the morning, and I knew I'd have to make this fast. I told her what I wanted, and why.

"Oh, Joe," she said when I finished, "I don't know about that. I don't know about that at *all*! I think we should ask Emma's permission before we simply—"

Another thump. The couch was moving into place.

"I don't want to argue about this, Jenny," I said. "I think it's necessary, and I don't think we need to talk to Emma about it. Not yet, anyway. I've told you what I'm looking for. Do you have any ideas on the subject?"

"Yes, I do—one moment." The noises had stopped, and I listened as she thanked the delivery people. At last I heard her apartment door close, and she came back on the line. "Okay, that's done. I'm actually sitting on my brand-new couch. Now, you're meeting Emma this afternoon, right?"

"Yes," I said.

"Okay, I have an idea, but it may take a while. Call me when you're finished with her. I should know something by then."

"What's your idea?" I asked.

She told me.

I thought about it. Why not? I decided. It was worth a try. "All right. I'll call you at about three o'clock."

"Good," Jenny said. Just before hanging up, she added, "You know, this is rather exciting!"

"What, your new couch?"

She laughed, and I joined her. "No, I mean *this*. I feel like—I don't know—like Nancy Drew!"

"Yeah. I'll call you later, Nancy."

• • •

The law firm of Gillespie and Martin was on the fifth floor of a big building on Madison and Fifty-seventh. I met Emma in the coffee shop in the lobby, as arranged, and we rode up in the elevator.

The suite of rooms into which we were ushered by a friendly young woman who took our coats was a great deal more modern looking than I had expected. The entire outer wall of the building was tinted glass, for one thing, and everything else strove to appear in harmony with the architecture. Beige walls and carpets, polished oak desks, traveling curtains of some rough-woven, wheat-colored material. Track lights dramatically hit the modern art everywhere: huge paintings and wall sculptures. I thought again of Sarah Masterson's apartment. Either her decorator was much in demand or this was the current rage. Perhaps *New York* magazine had been the arbiter of all this in a recent article, dubbing the look "retro-modernist," or something like that. I wouldn't put it past them: I hold that publication personally responsible for Amish quilt wall hangings, gourmet jellybeans, balsamic vinegar, *café latté*, and the curious box-office success of several truly dreadful foreign films. Maybe the whole Upper East Side looks like this nowadays, I thought. Then I remembered my mother's Fifth Avenue penthouse, patterned after a West Indian cottage, and smiled. My mom, the maverick. She wouldn't be found dead in this décor. Then again, most Upper East Siders wouldn't be found dead in hers—unless, of course, the West Indian thing gets revived by *New York* magazine, at which time the entire Upper East Side will look like a Carmen Miranda movie. I prefer my mother's taste, so there.

Emma looked good today, I noticed as the young woman led us through the suite. She was wearing a simply tailored navy blue suit with a white blouse, and her hair was up. I don't know much about women's clothes, but I know expensive when I see it. I also noticed a different mood today: she was unusually quiet, almost grave.

"I hate coming here," she whispered to me as we walked. "I hate talking about money."

That explained the mood.

We passed several secretaries and law clerks busy at their desks, a couple of small offices, an empty boardroom, and the closed, padded door to what I presumed was the lair of the partner named Martin. At last we arrived at the corner office, at another big, padded door. The receptionist threw open the door and led us in.

"Mrs. Smith and Mr. Wilder," she told the man behind the desk before departing, closing the door behind her.

"Hello again, dear," Daniel Gillespie said, rising and coming around from behind his desk. He and Emma embraced.

"Hi, Uncle Dan. Thanks for seeing us on such short notice."

Mr. Gillespie grinned. "Nonsense, dear. Hello, Joe. Come, sit down."

He led us over to a complete living room setting on one side of the room. The two far walls were tinted glass, with the now-familiar rough curtains opened to expose an enormous panorama. I could see up and down Madison Avenue, and most of Fifty-seventh Street as well. The two inner walls were lined floor to ceiling with oak shelves, and these were lined with what must have been every law book ever written. The paneled spaces between shelves were covered with framed sheepskin diplomas and certificates. The wheat and mocha-toned couch and armchairs and the coffee table between them provided a plush, comfortable room-within-a-room. I looked around the office, wondering how much of it was a result of Mr. Gillespie's association with the Masterson family.

Most of it, apparently. No sooner had we sat down than the door opened and another young woman arrived with a silver tray. A glass pitcher of iced tea, a saucer of lemon wedges, sugar and artificial sweetener, a plate of butter cookies, and three tall, *New York* magazine–sanctioned octagonal glasses.

Emma smiled for the first time.

"You remembered!" she cried, leaning forward to pour for us all as the girl slipped out of the room.

"How could I forget?" Mr. Gillespie said. "Ever since you were a little girl: iced tea and butter cookies after lunch!"

And that's how you entertain a trust fund baby.

I let her do all the talking. She simply informed her attorney that I was, at her request, looking into "certain matters" for her, and she asked him to explain the particulars of her finances to me, including the contents of her last will and testament.

Daniel Gillespie leaned back in his chair, tinkling the ice in his glass. " 'Certain matters.' May I ask, what is the nature of Joe's inquiry?"

Emma was ready for that one.

"I'll tell you later, Uncle Dan," she promised, smiling prettily. "For now, just tell him everything. Start with my great-grandfather."

To his credit, he let it go at that. He looked from Emma to me.

"Okay," he said at last. "Bradley Masterson was an iceman, the son of an iceman, here in Manhattan shortly after the turn of the century . . ."

It was an amazing story.

Bradley's father's actual last name had been O'Masters, and he'd fled an impoverished, blight-stricken Ireland for the promise of New York City at the height of the Industrial Revolution. He and his pale young wife, Nell, had decided to anglicize their surname even before Ellis Island appeared on the horizon. Even so, they'd only been able to find lodgings in the predominantly Irish section of the Lower East Side. Richard O'Masters, now Richard Masterson, had used what little money he had to buy a horse-drawn ice wagon.

He sold his wares all over lower Manhattan, and he soon began to look around for ways to expand. Nell died giving birth to Bradley in 1885, and Mr. Masterson never remarried, despite the availability of more than a few attractive widows and eligible young women. The little boy grew up helping his father with the business, and he took over the Masterson Ice Company, which had grown to fifteen wagons and a small office, when Richard died in 1912.

Bradley—Brad, as everyone called him—had been a husband and father in his early thirties, just after World War I, when he and a friend had come up with the idea of electric iceboxes. The friend, one Amos O'Connell, was one of the first professional electricians in New York City, and his hobby was dreaming up all sorts of projected gadgets that incorporated Mr. Edison's great discovery.

When Brad suggested the possibility of electric refrigeration, Amos was fascinated with the idea. He pondered long and hard, and by the time he and his wife died in 1926—in an electrical fire, of all things—he'd come up with a sleek design for what would eventually become the modern refrigerator, and he'd actually made notes for possible experimentation with hydrocarbons as a way to keep the box cold without resorting to ice. He was on the right track, as it turned out: years later, the connection was finally made by others, who discovered a way to fluorinate hydrocarbons to create Freon, the coolant used in refrigerators and air conditioners.

At the time of his friend's death, Brad had already patented his own design for iceboxes, and he was manufacturing and selling them on a modest scale. When he bought up a warehouse full of gas stoves at a liquidation sale, he put his brand name on them and sold them as well. Over the years he added lighting fixtures, electric heating bars, electric phonographs, and radios to his inventory. Masterson Appliances became one of the most popular businesses in New York. Not satisfied with that, Brad came up with a mail-order catalog, and soon he was selling his wares in most of the forty-eight states.

When the first electric kitchen appliances appeared, Brad remembered his friend's notes and sketches, locked away in the safe at his first warehouse. He handed the materials to the designers at his new plant in New Jersey, and three years later he had one of the best refrigerators on the market. Electric ranges, blenders, and percolators followed. His company was one of the first to advertise on television, although several more years would pass before televisions were manufactured by his company. At his death in 1955, his devices could be found in nearly every home, office, hotel, and restaurant in America.

Bradley Masterson's newfound, hard-earned fortune had one inevitable side effect: he became obsessively possessive of it. He gazed out from his big townhouse on Tenth Street—one of the streets in which his father had once driven his lone ice wagon—and vowed that his money, like his products, would always bear the name Masterson. Thus was born his unusual last will and testament.

His son, Bradley Junior, had died fighting in Europe, and his only grandchild was a girl. So be it, he thought: if not the name itself, at least a direct bloodline. He left the company to his wife, the first Laura, with instructions to her that she leave it to her granddaughter and namesake. Their daughter-in-law, Sarah Masterson, was well provided for with a trust fund. His will instructed all future heirs, beginning with Laura Masterson Vale, to likewise leave the fortune to the first son or, in the absence of male issue, the eldest daughter.

Laura had complied with his wish in her own will. When she was murdered sixteen years ago, the bulk of the estate and controlling shares in Masterson were left not to her husband, Walter, but to Emma. Walter, like Sarah Masterson before him, was given a considerable amount of money, and he was already president of the company. But he was merely a spouse, not a blood relative, so he could not inherit everything.

And that is how Emma Masterson Vale Smith became one of the richest women in America.

Emma's will, like her mother's, respected and perpetuated her great-grandfather's wish. In the event of her death, controlling interest in Masterson Electronics Corporation would be placed in trust for her first son or, barring that, daughter. If she died without issue, the entire estate would pass to her sister, Sarah Vale, who already had her own trust fund. Emma's husband, Stan, would receive a large annuity. There were small bequests to several friends, including Rachel Cohen and Jenny Hughes, and to certain charities. She further instructed that her father, Walter Vale, was not to receive anything.

If Sarah Vale inherited but died childless, Bradley's request of ownership by direct bloodline would no longer be valid. In the case of that remote possibility, the entire estate would be divided equally among the surviving spouses of direct descendants: currently Sarah Masterson, Walter Vale, and Stanley Smith.

Emma's unborn child didn't know it yet, but he or she was destined to be very, very rich. How fitting, I would later think, that Emma had already decided that if it was a boy, his name would be Bradley Masterson Smith. The old man would have danced a jig.

I sat there, slowly chewing the last of my butter cookie, staring out at the skyline beyond Daniel Gillespie's head. I had been hoping that this trip to the lawyer's office would clear things up for me, shorten the list of suspects. As it turned out, I realized, the fun was just beginning.

Emma thanked "Uncle Dan" for his time and hospitality, kissed him on the cheek, and led me out of the office and down to Madison Avenue.

"I must fly!" she cried as we emerged into the sunlight. "It's after three: I have to be at the chiropractor at four. I don't have time to get my car out of the garage. I'd better take a cab.''

I stepped from the curb into the street and raised my arm. Almost immediately, a bright yellow taxi pulled to a stop in front of us. As I was handing her in to the backseat, something occurred to me.

''Emma,'' I said, ''is your weekly appointment with your chiropractor every Monday at four?''

''Yes.''

''Do you usually take your own car?''

''Yes.''

I closed the door behind her and leaned down to the open window. ''And do you always take the FDR Drive?''

She laughed. ''Of course, silly! Always. That's the *only* way to get from here to the East Village.'' She turned away from me and spoke to the driver. ''207 East Ninth Street, please—and take the FDR.''

''Yes, ma'am.''

She smiled and waved to me as the car glided away and turned east on Fifty-seventh Street. I watched her go, thinking, yes. Routine. Predictability. She always drove herself. She always took the same route. She occasionally took sleeping capsules. She was allergic to aspirin.

Common knowledge.

That's how it can be done.

I frowned as I watched the taxi disappear, thinking, What else does she *always* do? . . .

With that thought, I stepped back onto the sidewalk and hurried over to the bank of pay phones on the corner.

When Jenny answered, I said, ''Hello, this is Mister Sherlock Holmes. I'd like to speak to Miss Nancy Drew.''

There is no laughter in the world as lovely as that of a West Indian woman. ''Speaking.''

''Miss Drew, I was wondering if you were successful in your latest bit of detection.''

More laughter. ''Where are you, Joe?''

''Fifty-seventh and Madison.''

"Well, hop in a cab and come over to my place. I did better than merely *detect*."

I was there in fifteen minutes, which any New Yorker will tell you is not bad for three-thirty on a Monday afternoon. The attractive red brick apartment building was just in from a corner on the north side of a pretty street facing Gramercy Park. The black wrought-iron fence on the south side encloses one of the loveliest patches of green in the city. Jenny's apartment, the front half of the second floor, had three big windows facing the square.

I rang the appropriate bell, announced myself to her, and was buzzed into a cool, quiet lobby. I didn't bother with the tiny elevator; I took the stairs beside it, arriving in a little foyer in the stairwell giving onto two doors, front and back. The front door was already open, and Jenny stood there, smiling at me.

"Hello," she said. "Welcome to my new home."

I smiled and stepped past her, into the room.

She had neither Sarah Masterson's decorator nor the current approval of *New York* magazine—but my mother could very well have helped her. Once they've lived in the Virgin Islands, many people have a tendency to make every place they inhabit thereafter a constant reminder. I stood quite still in the center of the living room, drinking in the exposed red brick front and side walls, the wicker ceiling fan, the rattan peacock chairs, the brand new white rattan couch with deep cushions in a bamboo print. Tall, potted tropical plants near the big front windows, all but writhing ecstatically in the sunlight pouring in on them. The deep area rugs were vividly textured in bold African designs. Two black mahogany ceremonial masks competed with the bright watercolors of familiar Caribbean scenes along the walls. I heard the faint trickle of water and looked down: a rectangular, metal pool-enclosed brook, with waterwheel spinning industriously, set with large stones and ringed with ferns, provided the base for her glass-topped coffee table.

She'd been here two weeks. After fifteen years, *my* apartment still had all the personality of a room at any Ramada Inn. I shook my head, smiling, before turning my attention to the blue peacock chair in the far corner.

The big, powerfully built man who sat there looked distinctly out of place in this distinctly feminine environment. He was a couple of years younger than I, I'd guess, maybe thirty-five, and he was definitely not someone you'd want to meet in a dark alley unless he was a friend of yours. He had a shaggy, shoulder-length mane of dark blond hair and a two-day stubble of beard. He slouched against the brightly colored cushions in ripped jeans, gray sweater, a battered leather bomber jacket, and scuffed, well-worn desert boots. He clutched a dark green Heineken bottle in his mighty fist, and there was a slight frown on his rugged face. He nodded curtly to me as I stepped toward him. Slowly, almost insolently, he stood up from the dainty chair, all six feet, four inches, and two hundred thirty pounds of him.

It occurred to me that we'd never been formally introduced. I'd only seen him a few times, briefly, in St. Thomas seven years ago, and our relationship then had not been conducive to casual friendship. But that was then, this was now. I stuck out my hand, grinning. After a moment, he grunted and extended his own. I could practically hear my knucklebones crunching together as we shook, but I managed to keep the grin on my face.

I said, ''Mr. Charles Lannigan, I presume.''

FIVE

Chap

"Chap," he said.

"I beg your pardon?"

"My name. It's Chap, not Charles. I hate Charles." He turned to Jenny, extending the Heineken bottle. "Got another one of these?"

"Sure," our hostess said. "How about you, Joe?"

"Nothing, thanks."

"Back in a minute," Jenny said, and she went into the kitchen.

I sat on the new couch, and the big blond man chose another chair—one that looked considerably sturdier than the peacock fan chair in the corner, which was probably a good thing. We regarded each other for a moment before I began.

"So—uh—Chap, has Jenny told you anything about this situation?"

He shook his head, settling back in the chair and bringing his right boot up to rest across his left knee. Then he looked at me, waiting.

"Okay," I said. "First of all, what exactly is your profession, if I may ask?"

Chap Lannigan shrugged. He thought a moment, then said, ''Protection.''

I smiled. I knew that much. Seven years ago in St. Thomas, he'd killed a man and nearly been killed himself, protecting me. ''I mean, what do you call yourself? Are you a detective, or—''

He uttered a low, growling sound that I interpreted as a laugh. ''Do I have an office, is that what you mean? What do I put under 'Occupation' on my 1040 form? Am I listed in the fuckin' Yellow Pages?'' He dropped the crossed leg to the floor and leaned forward. ''Listen, man, I just got a call from a guy, telling me that Jenny Hughes was here in New York and that she was looking for me. So I called her, and she told me about you, and she said you folks need some kind of help, and there's good pay in it. I come here and sit in some fancy chair and have a beer and ask her what's up, and she says wait till Joe gets here. Well, you're here, right? Now, how about you tell me what you want me to do, and I'll tell you whether or not I want to do it.'' With that, he leaned back in the chair again, and the right boot once more came up over the left knee.

Okay, I thought as Jenny came back into the room and handed him another Heineken. So be it. Jenny sat beside me on the couch, facing him, and I began.

I talked for a while, telling him everything I knew so far, and Jenny filled in other things. Chap Lannigan stared out the window throughout most of it, occasionally taking a pull from the bottle. Every now and then he'd grunt or nod his head, so I knew that despite his casual posture he was paying close attention to the story. He was not the sort of man to whom you had to repeat things.

When we were finished with our recitation, he asked, ''Where does she live?''

I told him.

He glanced down at his ripped, patched attire. ''Clothes.''

I laughed. ''Yeah, you'd stand out on Madison Avenue,

dressed like that. If you take the job, I can advance you some—''

He cut me off with a wave of his hand. ''One thing. Does this Emma Smith know about me?''

''No. This is entirely my idea.''

''Okay,'' he said. ''Do you *want* her to know about me?''

Jenny and I looked at each other. I wasn't sure what she was thinking, but I knew what I was thinking. Seven years ago in St. Thomas, this man had been hired to follow me and protect me, and I hadn't been told about it. When I became aware of his constant presence, I freaked. I thought he was one of the bad guys—which wasn't a bad guess, given his overall appearance. Emma Vale Smith would have the same reaction.

''Yes,'' Jenny said, answering for both of us. ''We're going to tell her about you. Right, Joe?''

''Right,'' I said.

''Right,'' said Chap Lannigan. ''That's the best way.'' He glanced briefly at me, and I detected a flash of humor in his eyes. He was remembering, too. Then he leaned forward, and his manner became surprisingly professional. ''Now, the guy who called me today said good pay. How good?''

I stared at him for a moment. I had a sudden, whimsical vision of this man—properly dressed, of course—at a dinner table with my mother. The funny thing was, she would adore him. Linda Wilder has always been honest and plain-spoken, and my sister Lee has inherited the trait. They also have a tendency to appreciate the trait in others. I knew at that moment that they would both like Chap Lannigan, and I realized that I was beginning to like him, too.

Jenny was looking at me, waiting for a decision. I nodded to her and turned to him.

When I told him what I would pay him to protect Emma Vale Smith, he didn't even blink.

But he nodded. Then he reached over and once more crushed my hand in his.

"Are you sure about this, Joe?" Jenny asked me the minute Chap Lannigan had gone. "I mean, I know you're not exactly on your way to the poorhouse, and I'm willing to split it with you, if you want, but, well, can you afford this? Maybe we should simply ask Emma to—"

"That won't be necessary," I said as firmly as I could, cutting off all further argument. "I told him what I'm paying him, and that's what I'm paying him. Don't worry about the money, Jenny. It isn't mine. I'm being—um— I'm being financed by a private source."

That was an understatement, and just about the lamest thing I'd ever said. I'd never told Jenny about the money I was about to inherit from a friend of ours or the bank account I was setting up with it. It was a long and complicated story, and I wasn't at all sure I wanted to repeat it. With any luck, she wouldn't ask me to explain.

"Would you please explain that?" Jenny said. "What do you mean, a private source?"

So much for my luck.

"Sit down, Jenny," I said, and she did.

Our new employee was off to "pick up some things," as he'd expressed it. I assumed this meant new clothes with the cash advance I'd given him. I wondered if it meant a gun, as well. Then he was going to Madison and Sixty-fifth to check out Emma's building. After that, he'd said, he'd be home waiting for further instructions. I had no idea where his home was: he hadn't volunteered that information.

"First of all," I said, "how did you find him?"

"Milton," she replied. Milton had been her personal bodyguard in the Virgin Islands, when her father was the governor there. "I called him in St. Thomas, and he gave me a number up here, so I called that. From the noise in the background, I'd say it was some kind of restaurant or bar. There was music, and what sounded like a pool game. The man who answered had some sort of accent, maybe Russian. I told him I was trying to get in touch with Charles Lannigan, and he took my name and number. Half an hour later, Charles—uh, *Chap* called me.''

"How is Milton these days?'' I asked, remembering the big, serious native man from seven years ago and wondering again whether Milton was his first name or his last name.

"He's fine. He's married now, with two children. He works for the new administration at Government House. He said to say hello to you.''

I nodded. "So, what do you think of Chap Lannigan now?''

"He looks like he did then,'' Jenny said. "Like someone who can handle just about anything. Now, tell me how you're paying him.''

So I told her.

Seven years ago, after the incidents in St. Thomas, one of my oldest friends disappeared from the face of the earth. As he had no relatives by that point, his considerable fortune was left to me. There is a seven-year statute of limitations on missing persons in the United States, after which the person is presumed dead. For my friend, that limit would be reached in about two weeks. I'd resigned myself to his disappearance, as I'd resigned myself to the fact that I would soon inherit fourteen million dollars.

It's considerably more than that now, if you add seven years of interest, closer to twenty million, but I'm assuming most of that goes in annual taxes. When it becomes mine, the inheritance tax will cut it in half, so I'm probably looking at a final figure somewhere between eight and ten million. Whatever it is, it's found money.

I was still recovering from the devastation in my hometown when I was informed of this legacy, and I decided that if I got the money, I would not use it for myself. I would establish a bank account, a fund, which I would use to help others in need. That is still what I plan to do.

Of course, I don't need a psychiatrist to tell me that I'm really guarding the fortune, keeping it safe on the off-chance that my oldest, dearest friend will one day reappear. I don't know whether he's dead or alive, and until I know for certain—well, that's where the money is.

Jenny listened in silence, and she offered no comment at the end. She merely nodded her head. I think it was the nod that made me decide to do what I'd been thinking about doing ever since she'd invited me to dinner more than a week ago. I'd been thinking about it a lot. I leaned forward.

"Jenny, you said you're not going to be teaching any-more, and you're here in New York looking for a new line of work. You don't have to decide now, but I'd like it if you would consider working with me."

She stared, clearly confused. "You're a writer, Joe. What do you need, some sort of secretary? Someone to retype your plays and novels? I don't—"

"No," I said, laughing. "That isn't the work I meant. I'm talking about *this*, what we're doing now for Emma. The fund I've set up. I'm calling it the Mongoose Fund, after the old story. It's for people in trouble, people who need help."

She knew the old West Indian fable as well as I did. We'd both been brought up on it. There are no snakes in the Virgin Islands, for the simple reason that the local mon-gooses got rid of them many years ago. But regional folk-lore throughout the world abhors simple explanations for things, and the Caribbean is no exception. According to the old people in the Islands, the mongoose is a mystical crea-ture, a sort of heavenly protector, able to drive evil from a place. When the last snake was destroyed, it is said, the mongooses gathered together and danced under the full moon, celebrating their victory.

"Oh," Jenny said. "So, you want to open a detective agency, is that it?"

"Not exactly. Nothing quite so formal. I don't know

what you'd call it, really. Just a—a place where people can
go when they don't know where else to go. Only they
wouldn't come to me—to *us*. We'd go to them.''

She gave me a bemused smile. ''So, you want to be like
Sherlock Holmes? A consultant, only taking the cases that
interest you?''

''Yes.''

''Are you going to give up writing?''

''No. It would be an occasional thing, I imagine. But,
because of the money, there could be two—or three—people involved. On a permanent salary.''

Jenny continued to stare. ''But if you don't advertise,
how will you find clients?''

I stood up, took her hand to pull her up from her chair,
and led her over to the nearest window.

''Look,'' I said. ''What do you see out there?''

The sun was setting, and the shadows in the street and
the park outside were lengthening. The street lights lining
her block had come on, and the bare branches of the trees
in Gramercy Park rustled in the wind. We could tell, from
the way the people below us were bent forward, clutching
the collars of their coats in their gloved hands as they
passed by, that the wind was sharp and bitterly cold. An
old man walking a tiny black dog was urging it along, and
he finally picked it up and hurried off. A woman with a
baby carriage was fairly running, pushing the pram before
her as fast as possible. Businesspeople, in suits and ties, on
their way from work. Children playing in the last light before going home to dinner. A young man and woman,
laughing, holding hands as they ran toward shelter.

''I see the world,'' she whispered.

''Yes. And there's a lot of bad stuff in it. I found that
out in St. Thomas, and so did you. I want to do something
about it, if I can. That's what I want to use the money for.
I won't have to look far, I imagine. You certainly didn't.
You only had to look as far as your friend, Emma. You

don't have to answer now, but I want you to think about my offer."

She was still looking out the window. "Why me?"

"Because you were there when it happened. You and I were victims. We are the only survivors."

She nodded after a moment, and I went to get my coat.

"But now," I said, "I'm taking you out to dinner, and then we're going to meet Mr. Lannigan."

SIX

Suspects and Cappuccino

He lived in the East Village, as it turned out.

After dinner in a nice Italian restaurant about a block from her building, we went back to her place to call him. No bartender this time: he'd apparently given us a home number. It was answered on the first ring.

"Yeah?"

"Hi, it's Joe Wilder."

"Yeah. What's up?"

"Did you see her place?"

"Yeah. Saw her, too."

"Did you introduce yourself?"

"No. Thought I'd leave that to you."

"Okay. You busy at the moment?"

"I guess you could say my time is yours."

"Good," I said. "Let's meet in an hour. We've got to come up with a plan."

"I can be there in an hour."

I looked around Jenny's apartment, thinking. Then curiosity got the better of me. "No, we'll come to you."

"Uh, I don't know—"

"Where are you?"

There was a pause. Then he said, "Second and Sixth, but I'm not, uh, prepared to entertain. There's a coffee place one block up, on the corner of Seventh Street, Mario's. I'll meet you there at ten."

"Right," I said.

Café Mario was across the street from a busy multiplex cinema, and there didn't seem to be a free table. I was looking around for someone to put us on a waiting list when a stunning young woman with long red hair materialized before us in the crowded room.

"You guys lookin' for Chap?" she asked us.

"Why, yes," Jenny said.

"This way, please." She turned and led us through the room to the back corner, to an empty table we hadn't noticed in the crowd. A white cardboard sign marked Reserved was whisked away, and we were seated and handed menus.

"I'm Amber," the girl told us. "You're Jenny, and you're Joe, right? Hi. He said go ahead and order, and he'll be along soon."

I ordered American coffee with milk and sugar, which made Jenny and the beautiful Amber giggle. Jenny ordered decaf cappuccino, which made *me* giggle, and we decided to split a chocolate pecan tart.

At exactly ten o'clock, Chap Lannigan came through the door, and, but for his height and build, we almost didn't recognize him. He wore a gray trenchcoat over a charcoal gray, double-breasted suit with a white shirt and blue-and-gray striped tie, and his shaggy blond mane was gone. In its place was a glistening, swept-back razor cut that must have set him back the better part of fifty bucks. The black shoes would have cost considerably more.

"What the hell—" I began before Jenny's swift kick under the table silenced me.

"Good evening, Chap," she said as he dropped into the

seat next to her. "This is a lovely place: I'm glad you suggested it."

He smiled and nodded to her. Amber arrived with our order, and I wasn't a bit surprised when she leaned down and kissed him on the cheek.

"Hi, Chap. Bitchin' suit. Your usual?"

"Yeah, babe, thanks."

His usual turned out to be American coffee. I withered Jenny with my smile of triumph as he added milk and sugar. She laughed, conceding with grace, and went back to her decaf cappuccino. I had been absolved of my crime, ordering actual coffee in a Greenwich Village coffeehouse. *New York* magazine strikes again.

"Okay," I said, "here's the situation. Emma Smith is in danger. At least, she says she is. Unless she hasn't told us something important about herself, I think we can come up with a short list of likely suspects. It's got to be someone close to her. Two reasons. First, she's filthy rich, and her death would benefit several people. Second, the aspirin. Anyone could have been in the car on the FDR Drive, but the aspirin incident was in her bathroom, on the night of the party.

"According to her, no one else was in her apartment for several weeks before the party except her housekeeper, her husband, and herself. No deliveries, no cable company, no telephone man. Nothing. The caterer is a friend of hers, the same company who caters Masterson functions. No aspirin was found in the sleeping pill bottle the next day. My guess is this: only one aspirin capsule was put into the bottle, and it was done during the party. It was just luck that she shook out that capsule that night. Of course, it would have been dropped on top of the other capsules in the bottle, so it isn't really so strange. Incidentally, I don't know that one aspirin would be enough to kill someone who's allergic, but it would definitely make them sick, which it did. If it wasn't an out-and-out murder attempt, it was definitely a threat of some kind."

I took a deep breath. "Now, what we need is a list."

"Ready," Jenny said. I looked over at her. She had produced her spiral notepad, and her pen was poised. Beside her, Chap Lannigan was staring off into the crowd behind me, but I knew he was listening. Like that afternoon, when he'd been staring out the window in Jenny's apartment. This was apparently his listening mode.

"You know these people, Jenny," I said. "Why don't you start us off here?"

"All right." She thought a moment, then wrote. "First and foremost: Stanley Smith."

Chap nodded. "It's usually the husband. It's his medicine cabinet: he'd know what was in it. He'd know that the sleeping capsules and the aspirin capsules looked alike. For anyone else, it was just a lucky break."

"Ah," I said, "but it may have been just that. We can't assume that the aspirin incident was premeditated, like the car incident. But you're right, the spouse *is* usually the most likely candidate. My only question is, why? Go on, Jenny."

She thought again. "Sarah Vale. No love lost between them, and she's the chief beneficiary. I can't see her doing it, though, especially the bit with the car. She was always the world's worst driver. Emma used to make jokes about it."

"That's very interesting," I said. "Next?"

"Well, there's Craig Davis. But what the hell would *he* gain from Emma's death?"

"Quite a lot," I said, "if he marries her sister. Besides, she threw him over. Twice. Maybe we're dealing with a crime of passion."

"Hardly," Jenny said. "Have you ever heard of a crime of passion that was so—I don't know, *calculated*? No, I think we should agree right now that financial gain is the most likely motive."

Chap nodded. I stared across the table at the two of them. "You know," I said, "I'm beginning to enjoy this.

Okay, we have the husband and the sister, and the ex-lover who is now the sister's lover. Who else?''

Jenny thought. ''I think we can rule out some people. Rachel and Dave Cohen, for starters. And Mrs. Masterson. She adores Emma, and she wouldn't gain anything.''

''Agreed,'' I said. ''Ditto the lawyer, Gillespie. He seems to be more of a father figure than her own father.''

''That wouldn't be too difficult,'' Jenny drawled. Then she looked up sharply. ''What about that? What about Walter Vale?''

I shrugged. ''I've never laid eyes on the man. You have, though. Tell us about him.''

Jenny began absently drawing little squiggly lines on one corner of the page before her. I noticed that she'd printed the word *SUSPECTS* in large capitals at the top, and she had listed three names: *Stanley Smith*, *Sarah Vale*, and *Craig Davis*. After doodling for a few moments, she added a fourth: *Walter Vale*.

''The word I'd use,'' she said, ''is patrician. That's what he looks like, and what he acts like. Tall, silver-haired, formal, rather cold. I never felt comfortable around him, the few times we met. Not too often, because he and Emma don't get along. But I went to a couple of parties at his house on Long Island, the house Emma grew up in. He was polite, and so was his wife, I guess, but . . .'' She shook her head.

''Yes,'' I said, ''but would he kill his daughter?''

Jenny laughed. ''Sure. Why not? Then all he'd have to do is bump off his *other* child, and he'd get—what was it?—one third of Emma's marbles. Of course, *then* he could see to it that his son-in-law *and* his mother-in-law also had car accidents or took medicine they were allergic to, and pretty soon he would *be* Masterson Electronics. Not just the president, mind you. The whole enchilada.'' She laughed again. ''I don't know, guys, but that seems like a real long shot.''

"Maybe," I said, "but keep him on the list anyway. I want to meet Walter Vale. Who else?"

Jenny shrugged again. "Unless there's a motive we don't know about, I'd say that's about it."

I looked at the four names she'd written. "Well, that certainly narrows it down . . ."

Chap Lannigan, of whom we're all growing fond, chose that moment to add one of his rare comments.

"You may be able to narrow it down even more," he said.

Jenny and I looked at each other, then turned to stare at him. He picked up his coffee cup, drained it, and raised a hand to signal to Amber. She was at his side instantly, refilling his cup. Then she refilled mine, checked that Jenny was okay, smiled around at us, and disappeared again. When she was gone, Chap leaned forward, his elbows on the table, and asked the question that got us all thinking. A lot.

"How many of these people were around sixteen years ago?"

As I said, we're growing fond of him.

I hadn't thought about that. Some detective, huh?

It was one of the biggest high society crimes of its decade, and it had the further allure of being suitably shrouded in mystery. Everyone, including the police, *assumed* they knew what had happened, but no one was ever certain. It had entered popular folklore in the forms of a segment on *60 Minutes*; at least two patched-together, instant true-crime books, one in hardcover and one a paperback original; and a best-selling, thinly disguised novel by a reputable author. The novel, *A Perfect Wife and Mother*, had been made into a two-part, four-hour television movie.

"Seems to me," Chap was saying, "that trouble just follows that family around."

I shook my head. "It's a closed case. That guy was a

violent drug addict, and Laura Vale was trying to break up
with him.''

''Yeah,'' he said, a slow grin lighting his face. ''I saw
the movie, too. Morgan Fairchild and Gregory Harrison.''

''Wait a minute!'' Jenny cried, throwing down her pen.
''What are you saying, that whoever's trying to harm
Emma had something to do with? . . .''

''I'm not *saying* anything,'' he corrected her. ''I just
think it's a little hinky that sixteen years ago the owner of
Masterson Electronics was killed, and now the new owner
of Masterson Electronics is being threatened. Lightning.
You know, twice. Same place.''

We sat there, the three of us, looking at each other and
thinking. Jenny picked up the pen again.

''Okay,'' I said. ''Game plan. Jenny: call Emma tomorrow morning and arrange for us to meet her ASAP. I want
to introduce her to Chap. Chap: I want her watched, and I
want her followed. Can you do that alone, or do you need—
uh—''

''Backup,'' he supplied. ''Don't know yet. If I do, I
know a guy.''

''Right. I'm going to make an appointment with Stanley
Smith—a business appointment. And someone should talk
to the sister and Craig Davis . . .''

''I'll get on that,'' Jenny said as she wrote. ''Anything
else?''

''Yeah, there's one more thing. We may need Emma to
help us swing it. I want to meet Walter Vale.''

They both looked at me. When Jenny spoke, her voice
was very low.

''What are you thinking, Joe?''

I smiled. ''I'm thinking that Chap may have a point.
About lightning striking twice.''

There wasn't much to do after that. We finished our coffee,
but no check was brought to us. Amber, with a smile, shook
her head when I asked for a bill, and she had a brief, whis-

pered conversation with Chap. I wasn't deliberately trying
to listen, but I did hear two things. She said "in about an
hour," and he nodded and said something that ended with
the word "Mozart."

Then the three of us made our way through the still-
crowded café and out into the chill evening. I hailed a cab
for Jenny, and Chap and I watched as it took off across
Seventh Street. Then he and I said good-night, and he loped
off down the block.

I was about to hail a cab for myself when curiosity got
the better of me. I waited until Chap Lannigan turned the
corner, pausing to wave a greeting through the door of a
bar as he did. Then I hurried down the block after him. I
arrived at the corner of Sixth Street just in time to see him
disappear through the door just in from the corner, next to
the saloon. I glanced through the open door of the bar and
smiled. Jenny had said that Chap's answering service
sounded foreign, maybe Russian. The huge, bearded man
behind the bar looked like all the Volga boatmen rolled
into one.

I crossed the street and stood in the shadows on the south
corner, looking up at the building directly above the bar.
After a moment the lights came on in the two windows on
the second floor, and Chap arrived to partially open one of
the windows. I looked at the seedy building, the seedy,
neon-festooned bar, the seedy block, nodding to myself. As
I walked away to find a taxi, I heard the faint strains of
music above the din of the rock tune from the bar's juke-
box. It was coming from his open window.

Mozart.

SEVEN

Next of Kin, Part One

Two days later, on Wednesday, I went to see Stanley Smith at his office near Wall Street, but the interrogation did not go as I had planned. In fact, it didn't take place at all. I'm learning something about being a detective, I guess. You can't always rehearse, because you often find yourself proceeding without a script, improvising. Sometimes it takes a lot of questions to get to the bottom of things, and sometimes you just have to go on instinct. A small detail, a little thing like a silver-framed photograph, will end up saving you hours of work.

The weather seemed to be warming up as March approached. There was actually sunshine that day, and the temperature reached the low fifties at about two-thirty in the afternoon, when I was coming out of the subway and looking around. I've always had trouble getting my bearings in that odd conglomeration of tall buildings at the southernmost end of Manhattan. I'm not sure why, but there's something confusing, disconcerting about it. It doesn't *feel* like New York to me. That's probably because my interest in things financial is on a level with my interest in bullfighting. I don't enjoy seeing animals harmed, and I don't enjoy endless talk of stocks and assets and money markets. There's something oddly distasteful about it: it doesn't seem to be proper conversation for ladies and gentlemen. Maybe it's just me. But fate had dictated that I would have to at least feign an interest in it, so there I was.

Of course, it wasn't my real reason for coming. I'd told Stanley, at Sarah Masterson's party and again on the phone when I'd called for an appointment, that I wanted to invest a hunk of change in the stock market and in government bonds, which was true. What I didn't tell him was that I wanted to see him alone, in his own element, and get a feel for him. I wanted to know whether he was a potential murderer. It's hardly a thing you can ask someone on the phone.

His office was on the fourteenth floor of one of those sleek, impersonal, glass-and-chrome monoliths a stone's throw from South Ferry. I adjusted my imaginary deerstalker and tweed cape as I thanked the elegant receptionist who announced me for her directions and made my way down the industrial gray-carpeted, perfectly heated hallway to the appropriate door. I was Joe Wilder, detective, and I was on the job, infiltrating the lair of Suspect Number One.

"Hi, Joe." Stanley Smith—Stan, I reminded myself—smiled as he rose to greet me. His tie was loose around his neck, and the jacket of his blue suit hung over the back of the modest executive chair in his modest office. His thick brown hair was slightly rumpled, and his sleeves were rolled up to the elbows. He had probably just come back from lunch, and already there was a mound of papers before him. Either he was a hard worker or he chose to give me that impression. Men who are secretly planning to murder their rich wives will go to great lengths to keep up appearances. Or so I imagined as he waved me into the seat across the desk from him, facing the view.

"Hello, Stan," I said. "How's Emma?"

Of course, I knew how Emma was, because Chap Lannigan had called to check in with me just as I was leaving to come here. He was stationed outside her building, as he had been since I introduced the two of them the day before. He followed her when she went out, keeping a respectful distance, and they both seemed to be getting used to the arrangement. But Stan didn't know this, and Emma had instructed that he was not to know. Not yet, anyway. I guess I just wanted to see him sweat, or—even better—burst into tears and blubber a confession.

"Oh, she's fine," he said, glancing over at the silver-framed photograph of her on one corner of his desk. I followed his gaze with my own. "Now, you said you're going to be inheriting some money. If you can give me an idea of the amount we're talking about, I think I can show you several options—"

"Excuse me, Stan," I said, pointing at the little hand-made cardboard sign propped up beside the picture. "What's that?"

The white card was rather crudely printed in pink and blue marker. Against a field of hand-drawn stars and balloons was written the date, "*AUGUST 24!!!*" I could guess what it was, but I wanted to hear him say it.

The Number One Suspect blushed, smiling.

"Due date," he said.

I stared, first at the sign, then at the picture of Emma smiling beside it, and finally at Stanley Smith. Into his eyes. After a moment, I nodded.

"Eight to ten million, after taxes," I said.

He raised his eyebrows in startled appreciation. "Oh. Well, then, I think the best plan for you would be a combination of things . . ."

We sat there for nearly an hour, talking about it. He showed me brochures and reports from various companies, and he scribbled notes occasionally, explaining that he would have a proposed portfolio for my inspection in a day or so. He even invited me to his club, with a promise to teach me to play racquetball. And all through that hour, my eyes traveled constantly back to that picture of that lovely

woman, and to the crude little sign that made him blush
with pride, thinking, Sherlock Holmes should have had it
so easy.

So much for Suspect Number One.

Jenny fared somewhat better in the suspect department. She
seemed rather proud of that fact when we convened at her
apartment at four o'clock that afternoon. She'd had lunch
with Sarah Vale in some trendy place on the Upper West
Side, and she definitely had news.

"Sarah and Craig are planning to get married!" she
cried, handing me a glass of designer water and dropping
onto the chair across from me. "In June. It's going to be
a relatively small affair, apparently, at Walter Vale's house
on Long Island. We're invited."

"That's nice," I drawled. "Does Emma know?"

"Yeah. Sarah called her last night. She said Emma actually seemed pleased. And their father and stepmother are
ecstatic. Mrs. Vale is planning the whole thing with Sarah.
Wedding dress, caterers, musicians, all that. So, where does
that put Sarah and Craig on the suspect list?"

"I'm not sure. How was Craig?"

"Oh, I didn't see him. He's working somewhere, if you
can believe it. It was a girls-only lunch. Actually, the marriage plans were my entrée to her. I've never really known
Sarah well, and I don't particularly care for her. But when
I called her, she blurted out her news, so it was easy to
invite her to lunch to tell me all the details. No woman on
earth would pass up that opportunity, no matter how casual
the acquaintance. And that's when my *real* detective work
began."

"What do you mean?" I asked.

"Well, *in vino veritas* . . ."

Jenny proceeded to tell me about lunch, and the rather
surprising information she'd gleaned there. When Sarah
Vale arrived at the restaurant, she didn't look quite as
pleased as Jenny had been expecting. In fact, she seemed

rather upset about something. They discussed bridal gowns and china patterns as they ordered omelettes, and Jenny asked for a carafe of white wine. She only had one glass herself: the rest found its way into Sarah's glass. By the time they ordered coffee, Sarah had revealed her one misgiving about the impending festivities.

Sarah suspected that Craig was seeing another woman. She didn't know anything definite, she informed her new close friend, Jenny, but she just had a feeling. That was the word Jenny said she used: "feeling." Craig had seemed devoted enough ever since moving in with her a couple of years ago, but there were certain things Sarah had noticed that he'd never quite explained, including some rather secretive telephone calls and frequent, unexplained disappearances. When she'd suggested marriage—"Yes," Jenny explained, "*she* asked *him*!"—Craig had agreed readily enough, but he'd mumbled something about some "business" he would have to "take care of" beforehand. At first, Sarah told Jenny, she'd thought he must mean family business, but now she wasn't so sure.

"Of course," Jenny concluded, "I told her to confront him, to simply ask him if there was anyone else, or any other reason they shouldn't get married now. But she said no, she couldn't do that. So she's just going ahead with her plans." Jenny shrugged and leaned back in her brand-new rattan chair. "I don't know, Joe. She seems to be happy about the wedding, but, at the same time, she's rather worried. Some women are so insecure, especially women who, well, aren't especially pretty and have men who look like Craig Davis in their lives . . ." She trailed off, shaking her head.

"Hmm," I said.

Jenny raised her eyebrows. "What does that mean?"

"Well," I said slowly, "I'm not sure, but this is all very interesting. I wish Craig had been with you at lunch—but, then again, I don't suppose you would have heard all this if he'd been there. Still, I definitely think he's a better pos-

sible suspect than Sarah. I've only seen her once, but
Emma's description of her seems appropriate, not to mention your assessment. She struck me as being rather insecure, rather unsure of herself. In fact, I wouldn't be truly
surprised if she's wrong about another woman. Women like
Sarah are always imagining other women. Then again, men
like Craig always seem to have them. At any rate, I don't
think a murder plot would occur to her.''

"But you think it would occur to Craig?"

"That," I said, "is what I'd like to find out . . ."

Then I told her about my meeting with Stanley Smith,
and why I'd pretty much dismissed him as a likely suspect.
When she heard about the sign beside the photograph, she
agreed with me.

"So," Jenny said, "what now?"

I smiled. "Well, Nancy Drew, I think we should find a
way for me to see Craig Davis again. And I also want to
meet Walter Vale."

As it turned out, I never saw Craig Davis again.

I did meet Walter Vale, however, just a couple of days
later, but no one could have planned the circumstances of
our meeting. Well, that's not true: actually, somebody *did*
plan it, but it wasn't one of us.

EIGHT

Original Cast Album

It was a dark and stormy night...

The freezing rain began at midnight, and it was still pelting my windows two hours later. I closed the book, set it down on the coffee table, and turned my head to gaze into the flames. The plastic log in the fireplace was burning down now, and the hissing radiator was providing the actual heat in the room. I huddled in the armchair in my thick terry robe and slippers, sipping coffee and smoking a cigarette as I thought back over everything I'd learned in the last few hours.

The night sixteen years ago had indeed been dark and stormy. Much like tonight, I imagined as I glanced over at the windows, only it had been the middle of September, not the last week of February.

I don't know; I guess I just don't have an inquiring mind. That's obviously not true, but it isn't *that* kind of curiosity. I'd met Sarah Masterson at the ballet a couple of times, even dined with her, and I was vaguely aware of the tragedy in her family. I had never been particularly interested in it, and my mother and I had never spoken to Mrs. Mas-

terson about it. As Mom would be quick to point out, bringing up such subjects is simply not *done*.

But that was another country, as another playwright once
observed, and, besides, the wench was dead. If there was a
connection between sixteen years ago and the present, it
was important that I find it.

With a long sigh, I turned my attention from the fire to
the coffee table. The paperback I had just discarded was
titled *Beauty and Her Beast: The Death of Laura Masterson
Vale*. It was a slapdash job of reportage culled from published news articles, official records of the Oyster Bay and
Nassau County police, and courthouse documents of the
brief coroner's inquest. Dolores Trent, Michael's mother,
and two homicide detectives had actually spoken to the
book's author, but the Masterson-Vale family and their
friends and associates had apparently refused to contribute
to the enterprise.

The eight-page photo section in the middle of the book
showed me very young versions of Emma and her sister,
as well as pictures of virtually all the other major players.
Blond, elegant-looking Laura Vale herself, in the famous
Avedon photo-portrait and, more casually, grinning up from
a crowded round table in what the accompanying caption
informed me was the main dining room of the local beach
and yacht club. A considerably younger Laura stood smiling in her wedding gown, a handsome, dark-haired Walter
beside her. A far less flattering shot of Walter Vale, nearly
twenty years older, emerging from the courthouse with his
mother-in-law and his two daughters after the verdict of
murder/suicide had closed the book on the official investigation. A shot of the house on the headland in Cold Spring
Harbor, and two pictures of the poolhouse, interior and exterior. The interior shot showed a pleasant room with a
fireplace and attractive furniture, with two dark stains near
each other on the otherwise immaculate floor in front of
the couch.

The four photos of Michael Trent were pretty much what

I expected. A laughing ten-year-old in front of a tract house in an obviously unfashionable section of Tampa, a tired and rather grim-looking brunette woman in a nurse's uniform behind him, her hands on his shoulders. A husky high schooler in a football uniform, ball in hand, rearing back to throw a pass. The grinning, nude beach shot I remembered from the newspapers at the time, with long hair and sideburns, flexing powerful arms and chest, a discreet black bar censoring his midsection. And, last but not least, the tandem front-and-side mug shots of his angry face, a placard with a long line of numbers below his neck. The Tampa Police Department shots, taken at his arrest for assaulting a fellow lifeguard. An argument over a woman, according to the book, for which he'd spent a week in jail and lost his job. Shortly after this he'd come north, to Long Island. To the new job at the private beach club, the one in the picture, where he'd met Laura Vale.

The true crime book lay on my coffee table beside the novel, *A Perfect Wife and Mother*. I hadn't read it when it was a best-seller twelve years ago, nor had I seen the TV movie, but I'd thumbed through the paperback tonight. The names had been changed, of course, and the locale moved from Oyster Bay to Glen Head, but the basic facts were similar—and much easier to read than the dull, uninspired "true" account. Of course, there was no one alive to verify whether the poolhouse and the beach club had indeed been the sites of all that constant, sweaty, clinically described grappling between the two main characters, but at least the novelist, unlike the journalist, had a lively style. His final scene between "Lisa Dale" and "Mitchell Kent" in the poolhouse, with the drugs and the gun and the pleading, owed more to Act Five of *Romeo and Juliet* than to anything that ever took place.

That's easy for me to say, now that I know what really took place in the poolhouse. Oh, well . . . I looked again at the photos of Laura Vale and Michael Trent in the true crime book. Their fictional counterparts had been played by

Morgan Fairchild and Gregory Harrison, whom they
strongly resembled. I shook my head, remembering that
Emma was the image of her mother and Craig Davis looked
like Rock Hudson. Everybody was very attractive. Well,
almost everybody . . .

Both the fiction and the nonfiction books agreed with the
newspaper photocopies, or printouts, or whatever they
were, that Jenny had brought from the library. She'd spent
the better part of that afternoon looking through old files
from the *New York Times* and *Newsday*, which had quietly
and soberly related the facts of the case. She'd even thrown
in a few gushing, sensational front page headlines from the
New York Post and the *New York Daily News* ("HEIRESS
AND BEACH BOY IN FATAL LOVE NEST!" was the least in-
decorous of them).

In all of these accounts, even the novel, there were no
discrepancies. Nothing stood out in any way. Laura Vale's
diary confirmed that she and Michael Trent had met at the
beach, had been secret lovers for a year, and had frequently
argued. She'd blamed his moodiness on drugs, principally
cocaine. And her final entry on September 14, perhaps an
hour before she died, stated plainly that she was meeting
him to break it off that night. Well, as plainly as her ab-
breviated writing style would allow. In the middle section
of the "true" book there was a facsimile, a photocopy of
the final entry, in her sloping, graceful hand:

> "9/14—11:20 pm—Tonight's the night. Meeting M at
> poolhouse at 12. Telling him NO MORE. I can't go on
> like this. If W ever found out, it would kill him. I love
> W. WHAT AM I DOING?!! It's the right thing to do, the
> only thing to do. A just said so, and I agreed. 11:30.
> Oh, God, half an hour. Thirty lousy minutes! Thunder
> and lightning. I wish this rain would stop. I'm going
> mad. More later."

Of course, there had been no "more later." She ran out
into the storm, to the poolhouse, and that was the end of

that. I tried to imagine the scene between them, as the novelist had done, but all I could come up with was a lot of
indistinct yelling followed by two gunshots. I had no idea
what they would have been saying, but even then I didn't
put too much stock in the novel's overripe dialogue.

I looked at the diary entry again, wondering who *A* was.
M was Michael and *W* was Walter. But then came that
sentence: *"A just said so, and I agreed."* Then I remembered that Laura had just been on the phone with her
mother, Sarah Masterson, and her friend, Mrs. Nevins. I
paged back through the book to the chapter covering the
inquest. Mrs. Nevins's first name was Annemarie. So,
Laura's friend had known of the affair, and even advised
her about it.

Walter Vale, on the other hand, claimed to have known
nothing of the affair before the bodies were found. He
stated at the inquest that he had last seen his wife in the
living room at approximately 10:45, when he went up to
bed. She was still on the phone with Mrs. Nevins, he said,
and Mrs. Nevins's testimony confirmed this. Walter had
taken a sleeping pill, slept soundly through the night, risen,
had coffee in the kitchen, and left for work in the city just
before 8 A.M. He'd wondered why Laura was not with him
in bed when he'd awakened that morning. In the kitchen,
he'd asked the maid, Hannah Melton, where Mrs. Vale was,
and the girl had replied that she didn't know, she hadn't
seen her yet. Walter was at his office on Lexington Avenue,
and the two daughters were in school, at 12:45 that Thursday afternoon, when the maid had gone to the poolhouse
to collect the bathroom towels for the laundry. It was she
who had found the bodies.

Dolores Trent told the journalist who wrote the book that
her son had always been a good boy, a devoted son, but
that he'd always had his father's short temper. She blamed
Michael's troubles with women and drugs on that, including the incident with the other lifeguard in Tampa.

Why, I'd wondered as I read the factual accounts and

the glamorized version of Michael Trent in the novel, did
the mothers of dangerously unstable psychotics invariably
describe them as good and dutiful children? If Michael
Trent had been either good or dutiful, none of this would
have happened.

Now, as I stared down at the books and clippings on the
coffee table, that thought struck me again, only this time I
concentrated on it. Michael Trent, I thought. Michael Trent.
But for him, none of it would have happened. None of it . . .

There's no sight like hindsight. I almost grasped it then:
I almost made the connection. Sixteen years ago, and the
present . . .

I didn't make the connection, of course. Not then. If I
had—well, I don't want to think about that.

On that dark and stormy Thursday night, the last Thursday in February, I swept the clippings and the paperback
books together and tossed them in a drawer. Then I went
to bed.

Sherlock strikes again.

The following morning, Friday, I was awakened by the
ringing of the telephone. It was Emma, and she sounded
nervous.

"Hello, Joe. Listen, I'm—I'm having a bit of a problem.
I'll be at my office today, but I'll be home around four
o'clock. Could you come over then?"

"What's wrong, Emma?"

There was a slight pause before she replied. "I'd rather
not discuss it on the phone. I'll see you here about four,
okay?"

"Okay, but—"

She hung up before I could pursue it.

I called Chap Lannigan immediately. He answered the
cellular phone I'd given him on the first ring.

"Yeah?"

"Hi. Where are you?"

"Lobby of her building. What's up?"

"I'm not sure," I said. "She just called me. She said she's having a problem."

"Hmm. You want me to go up and talk to her?"

"No, I don't think so. She's getting ready for work right now. I'm coming there to see her when she gets home, about four."

"I'll stay close to her," he said.

"Good. I'll see you this afternoon."

The first thing I noticed was the music.

I'd checked in with Chap in her lobby before coming up. He'd walked with her to work and back, and he'd spent most of the afternoon in the reception area of Masterson's main offices on Lexington and Sixty-first. Now he was camped out on a chair in the lobby, reading. I glanced at the cover of his book: *Madame Bovary*. Emma had recommended it to him, he said. First Mozart, now Flaubert. Shaking my head in wonder, I'd waited while the doorman announced me before getting into the elevator.

She was in her work clothes, a blue suit and white silk blouse. Her hair was up, and she had on the obligatory war paint, that high-gloss makeup many female executives affect. She was holding a glass of iced tea when she opened the door. Despite her immaculate appearance, she seemed pale and drawn, as if she'd had a particularly challenging day at the office. But I didn't think so. She'd sounded pale and drawn, or whatever their auditory equivalents are, when she'd called me that morning. She was apparently worried, or annoyed, or both.

I recognized the music immediately. It emanated from the Masterson home entertainment center in the living room. It was the album of songs from the Broadway musical *Lady in the Dark*, which is a favorite of mine. I own this recording as well. As Emma stepped aside and waved me into the room, Gertrude Lawrence was socking out "The Saga of Jenny," the delightful bump-and-grind number about the vexating woman who always made up her mind—always with amusingly disastrous results.

It seemed appropriate to me that she would like this particular musical. It is the story of a rich and powerful woman
who finds herself at a crossroads in her life. The shadows
of the past, of certain incidents in her childhood, have led
her to the then-daring idea of psychoanalysis. There is one
specific memory she reveals under hypnosis, a fragment of
a song that apparently is of great importance to her. But
she can't remember it all, only the first few bars. It isn't
until the end of the play, when she has faced her demons
and found true love, that the entire melody is recalled. It is
the haunting Kurt Weill–Ira Gershwin ballad "My Ship."

She brought me a glass of iced tea and sat beside me on
the couch. We sat there for several minutes, listening to the
silly tale of the unfortunate "Jenny"—so dramatically different from our own Jenny. Finally, Emma turned to me
and spoke.

"I'm sorry if I alarmed you on the phone this morning,
but I don't know how much more of this I can take."

I stared at her. "How much of what?"

"Your friend, Mr. Lannigan. Chap. I mean, he's very
nice, and so forth, but I'm just not used to this—this constant scrutiny."

Oh, I thought. So *that's* it. "Excuse me, Emma, but it
was *you* who told *us* about the attempts on your life. Whoever it is, they could try it again at any time. I'm trying to
establish who it is, but until then I—"

"Oh, I know all that." She waved her hand dismissively.
"I know you and Jenny and Mr. Lannigan only have my
best interests . . . et cetera. But he's just always—*there*, you
know? On the corner, in the lobby, following me wherever
I go. I think Stan almost noticed him yesterday, when he
followed us to the restaurant and back. And I can't have
that. I can't have Stan . . ."

She trailed off, but I could fill in the rest. She didn't
want her husband to know about it. We were back to
Square One.

"What do you want me to do, Emma?" I asked.

At that moment, the funny song about Jenny making her mind up ended. There was a pause, and then the haunting melody began. "My Ship." Emma turned her head away from me, but not before I saw the single tear trickle slowly down her cheek.

"I don't know, Joe," she whispered as Gertrude Lawrence began the plaintive refrain. "I just don't know anymore."

We sat there in silence. The song continued softly in the background, the lady in the dark dreaming of the day when her ship would come in, bringing her gold and spice and rubies, knowing that it didn't matter unless her own true love was aboard as well. I couldn't think of anything to say to her, this beautiful, previously carefree young woman who was expecting a child. Who was trying to make a life with her husband. Who had never until recently even entertained the notion that there were people in the world who might envy her enough to wish her harm—if, indeed, that was the motive behind all this. But even then I think I knew that it was.

Then the song came to an end, and the recording with it. I sat beside her for a long time, watching her staring off at nothing, sipping her tea, as the shadows lengthened across the room. Finally, I broke the silence.

"I want you to tell me everything you remember about your mother," I said.

She turned to look at me. She studied my face for a moment. Then, with a little nod of her head, she began.

She spoke for a long while. She had adored Laura Vale, and she had not known very much about her. The events of September 14, sixteen years ago, had sent her into a profound state of shock. She'd recovered slowly, as time went on, but—here she smiled ruefully at me—she knew that, in some way, she would never fully recover from it. Her sister had recovered, quickly and easily, and that was part of what she disliked about her. As for her father . . .

According to Emma, Walter Vale was directly responsible for his wife's tragic fate. ''He all but ignored her, as
far back as I can remember. He was the president of Masterson, and he had all these business associates, and he was
always traveling. He took her for granted, I see now, though
I didn't know the meaning of that phrase when I was little.
But, looking back, I'd say that was exactly what he did.
He just always expected her to be there. Well, he was in
for a surprise—we *all* were. If he'd been a more attentive
husband . . . well, none of it would have happened. I'm certain of that.''

I wondered if she was perhaps being unfair to her father.
She'd been a child, and children don't always see everything. On the other hand, it's been my experience that children miss surprisingly little. It may have been that thought
that prompted my next question.

''Emma, did you know, or even suspect, about your
mother and Michael Trent?''

She shook her head. ''No, never. I mean, I knew he was
the pool lifeguard at the club, but we kids rarely went to
the pool. We were always on the beach. Mother and her
girlfriends hung out at the pool. I guess that's how she and
Mike—well, you know. But I had no idea that they were
lovers, and neither did Sarah. Nobody knew—until that
day, when the principal came and got me out of class . . .''
She trailed off, shaking her head again.

Though she was facing away from me, I knew that she
was crying again. I waited a few moments before asking
my final question.

''How do you feel about your mother now?''

There was another pause before she replied. She was
considering the question, and I got the distinct impression
that she'd never considered it before. At last she turned to
face me.

''I love her,'' she said. ''I miss her. Now that I'm old
enough, I think I understand her—certainly better than I
did at the time.'' She nodded, confirming to herself as well

as to me that this was true. Then she said, "I wish she were here now, even if it was just for a moment, so I could tell her that I forgive her."

I stared at Emma Vale Smith, appreciating again the horrible consequences of a guilty conscience. When she was fifteen, she'd learned truths about her mother in the worst way possible. And her fifteen-year-old reaction, after shock and grief, was a bitter feeling of betrayal. As she'd grown older and wiser, that feeling had been replaced by its inevitable replacement: guilt. Guilt for having felt betrayed in the first place, for having even briefly hated a mother who had suffered a violent death. It was a terrible burden, even now.

She was weeping again, and there was nothing I could think to say that would comfort her. And I certainly would not tell her today about my recent suspicion, that the old case and the new one might somehow be related. I would save that for another, more appropriate time. I rose to leave.

"I'm sorry, Joe," she whispered, reaching up with a hand to brush away her tears. "I don't let myself think about her very often, and when I do . . . oh, well . . ." She stood up, too, and I could see by her little smile that she was making a conscious effort to bring her emotions under control. "Thank you for coming over."

"Of course," I said. Remembering the original topic, her real reason for asking me here, I added, "Do you want me to call off the surveillance?"

She stared at me blankly for a moment. Then, obviously remembering Chap Lannigan's presence in her lobby, she smiled and shook her head.

"No, don't do that. I—I appreciate what you're doing, what *he's* doing. I just want all this to be over, you know?" She shrugged, and I saw another brief smile. "But until it *is* over, I guess I'd rather have Chap Lannigan nearby."

The very next day, Saturday, she and I both had reason to be grateful for her decision.

It happened on the exit ramp from the Brooklyn Bridge. Emma and Stan were in her car, and Emma was driving. They were on their way to their usual Saturday dinner with Stan's family in Cobble Hill. Chap was following them at a discreet distance. Traffic on the bridge going toward Brooklyn was relatively light at that hour: heavy traffic at that time is on the other side, as people pile into Manhattan for Saturday night activities.

It happened so fast that Chap didn't see it clearly. There were two cars between him and them, and he had just followed Emma's lead and put on his turn signal, preparing to turn onto the exit ramp, when a large black car streaked by him on his left. Emma was just going into the turn when the black car rammed into her left rear bumper. Chap heard a loud thud as Emma's car smashed into the concrete wall directly between the bridge road and the exit ramp. The drivers of the two cars behind hers slammed on their brakes and swerved to avoid colliding with her, and both cars immediately stopped, cutting off both bridge lanes. The black car—a four-door sedan with tinted windows was all Chap remembered—never even reduced speed. With the two stopped cars effectively cutting off any chance of pursuit, it simply disappeared down the road.

Chap hit his brakes and was out of his car and running toward Emma's in a matter of seconds, punching in emergency numbers on his cellular phone as he ran. He'd already summoned the police and paramedics before he reached them. The front of the car was completely caved in, and the windshield was broken. Black smoke was billowing from under the hood. The driver's-side air bag had inflated, and Emma was pinned behind it, screaming. Stan was sitting beside her, strapped in his seat belt but obviously unconscious. The driver's-side door was jammed shut by the impact, so Chap ran to the passenger side. He unstrapped the bleeding Stan and pulled him out onto the road, then jumped in to get Emma. She was still screaming when he reached her, so he slapped her hard across the face

and shouted instructions. She immediately shut up and un-
hooked herself, and he pulled her across the passenger seat
and out of the car. Taking Emma by the hand and lifting
the inert Stan with his other arm, he shouted to the other
motorists to get away from the car. Everybody obeyed him
and ran, which is why they were all at a reasonably safe
distance a few seconds later, when Emma's car exploded
and burst into flames.

NINE

Next of Kin, Part Two

Jenny and Mrs. Masterson had already joined Chap in the waiting room by the time I arrived at the hospital. The three of them were sitting, still and silent, in one corner of the big, crowded, ominously quiet room. Jenny was holding Sarah Masterson's hand, and the elderly woman was very pale. Chap had a fresh bandage on his left hand. When I asked him about it, he mumbled something about cutting himself on glass while getting Emma out of the car. Then he stood up and motioned me away from the two women.

In the hallway outside the room, he told me about the black sedan. Mrs. Masterson was under the impression that it had been an accident. We decided she could remain under that impression a while longer. The police already knew the truth from Chap and the other motorists, none of whom had gotten a license plate number, or even a very good look at the car. They all agreed that it was probably American. Chap thought maybe it was a Lincoln, but he couldn't swear to it.

Emma was apparently okay, Chap told me, but Stan was being worked on. That's as much as they had been told at that point. By the time we came out of the hallway to rejoin the women, a doctor in green scrubs was standing over them, talking in a low voice.

Stan was still unconscious, the result of a concussion. The right side of his head had struck the passenger door in the crash. Emma had a few cuts and bruises. She was being x-rayed and tested, and Stan was in surgery. The doctor hurried away, and the waiting in the waiting room resumed.

I hate waiting rooms. Well, I hate hospitals, period. With the exception of births, I can't think of anything nice that goes on there. They're like police stations: you only find yourself in one when something bad has happened. I couldn't sit still, as the others were doing, so I went outside. I paced the sidewalk near the front entrance in the cold early evening, smoking cigarettes and watching the grim arrivals and departures until Chap came out to get me.

Our group in the waiting room had grown considerably. I was introduced to Mr. and Mrs. Smith, Stan's parents, and two men about my age who were his brothers. One of the brothers had his wife with him, and she clutched the hand of a fidgety little girl. Within minutes of my return, Rachel and Dave Cohen joined us, followed almost immediately by Sarah Vale.

Chap and I were neither family nor friends, so we stayed off to the side, a little apart from the others. The last thing we needed was a high profile, relatives wondering why we were there. The Smiths sat with the elder Sarah, and Rachel and Jenny talked quietly with Stan's brothers. The little girl continued to fidget. The younger Sarah made several trips to the bank of pay phones nearby, coming back each time to announce that she couldn't locate Craig anywhere. Rachel and Jenny were just asking if anyone wanted anything from the refreshment machines when Walter Vale arrived.

I recognized him from the photographs I'd seen two nights before. I knew that he was in his early sixties, but he appeared to be considerably younger. He was a handsome man, as Jenny had said, tall and silver-haired and patrician, and in better shape than many men half his age.

The belted gray coat and black suit added to the impression
I had of great power and formality. I studied him as he
approached us down the long hallway.

The woman beside him was obviously the second Mrs.
Vale. She was about forty-five, and nearly as tall as he.
Short, dark hair and a black-and-red patterned scarf at her
throat were the only bold colors I noticed about her. She
was clad, head to toe, in white. Coat, suit, shoes and hat
were as immaculate as fresh snow. As they came nearer, I
saw that she was strikingly attractive, with large, dark eyes,
generous mouth, and high cheekbones. They were a very
handsome couple.

The two Sarahs, Mrs. Masterson and her granddaughter,
rose to greet them. Young Sarah embraced her father and
kissed her stepmother. Mrs. Masterson nodded rather stiffly
to the two of them before quietly telling them the most
recent news about Emma and Stan. When he heard that his
daughter was not seriously injured, Mr. Vale visibly relaxed.

What followed was a study in perfect manners born of
good breeding, as the two families shook hands all around
and murmured sympathetically. Mr. Vale was less reserved
when he greeted Jenny and Rachel Cohen. He remembered
them both fondly, apparently.

Then it was my turn. Jenny introduced me to the Vales,
both of whom smiled politely and shook my hand. I was
just beginning to wonder how to present Chap Lannigan
(''Mr. Vale, this is your daughter's bodyguard . . .''), when
the doctor arrived again.

''Mr. Smith is going to be fine,'' he said brightly. ''He's
conscious, and we want to keep him overnight for obser-
vation, but—''

''Can we see him?'' Stan's mother asked.

''Yes, of course, as soon as we get him settled in his
room. Just a few—''

''What about my daughter?'' Walter Vale interjected.

The doctor didn't get a chance to reply. There was a

shout from the corridor behind him. We all turned as Emma
came running down the hall, followed by a nervous-looking
nurse.

"Now, Mrs. Smith, you really shouldn't be running like
that! You've just been—"

Emma paid not the slightest attention to the woman as
she rushed forward into her grandmother's arms.

Ninety minutes later, only Jenny, Mr. and Mrs. Vale, Sarah
Masterson, and I remained in the waiting room. Emma had
greeted and been fussed over by all and sundry, and shortly
after that a nurse had arrived to announce that Stan was
ready for visitors. Emma and his family went away to see
him, and the crowd had eventually dispersed. The Cohens
left first, followed by Sarah Vale, and I signaled to Chap
that he should go, too. People were obviously beginning to
wonder who he was, and I couldn't come up with a satis-
factory explanation for his presence.

I watched Chap Lannigan depart, knowing that I would
have to deal with him soon. He'd been unusually quiet all
evening, even for him. I didn't know him well, but I could
see that something was bothering him.

The Smiths left after seeing Stan. The rest of us didn't
see him: he'd been through enough without a flock of relative strangers trooping in and out of his room. Now Emma
was alone with her husband, and the few of us who were
left were waiting to see what she wanted to do next.

I was beginning to wonder what *I* was going to do next.
I'd been working on a theory, and today's incident had
either reinforced it or blown it to pieces. I wasn't sure
which. I'd have to think about it soon, but not now.

Jenny was talking to the Vales, so I joined the conversation. Mrs. Vale, used to being a hostess, made it easy.

"So, Mr. Wilder," she said, "Jenny tells us you and she
grew up together in St. Thomas."

"Uh, yes," I replied. Not exactly true: we'd both grown
up on the island, but we'd barely known each other before

seven years ago. "Everybody calls me Joe."

"Okay, Joe," Mrs. Vale said. "I'm Ann. I've seen, let's
see, two of your plays off-Broadway. I'm afraid I haven't
read your novels yet."

"You have a treat in store," Jenny said.

I smiled.

"I always wonder how to return such compliments," I
told Mrs. Vale. "My kitchen fixtures are all Mastersons,
but they were there when I moved in, so I guess it's my
landlord's flattery. But I must say they've always worked
splendidly."

I was rewarded by a smile from her and laughter from
her husband.

"Well, I'm always glad to meet a satisfied customer,"
Walter Vale said, "even after all these years. I suppose it's
how you feel when people say they like your plays. I particularly enjoyed the comedy, *Me Again*. I don't have time
to read, however—unless you count contracts and brochures."

Everyone laughed. I watched him as I smiled. Yes, he
was charming. They both were.

"Speaking of contracts," Mr. Vale continued, looking at
his watch, "I'm afraid I must be going home—as soon as
I see Emma again."

"Business on Saturday?" Mrs. Masterson asked. I
couldn't help admiring her. I knew her relationship with
this man had cooled since her daughter's death and his
remarriage. She'd managed to ask a perfectly innocuous
question in a way that suggested subtly that perhaps his
daughter's welfare wasn't the most important thing in the
world to him.

If Walter Vale was aware of the implied slight—and I
was certain he *was* aware of it—he gave no indication.

"Oh, yes," he said, smiling again. "No rest for the
weary. I'm leaving for Tokyo on Monday, and we're getting papers ready over the weekend." He turned to his former mother-in-law. "The Sunyoki takeover. As a principal

stockholder, Sarah, you've certainly been following it?''

Touché. He'd met her subtle thrust with an admirable parry. Families, I thought. You gotta love 'em.

"Of course, Walter," was all Sarah Masterson could say.

They and the elegant Mrs. Vale were smiling away at each other when Emma—who, with her sister, constituted their only possible common ground—rejoined us.

"Here I am!" she announced brightly as she came up to us.

"And not a moment too soon," Jenny Hughes murmured. I was the only one who heard her, and I stifled an involuntary laugh.

"Stan's okay," Emma said. "He just asked for food, so that's a good sign. I'm supposed to come get him tomorrow morning."

"Is there anything—?" Ann Vale began.

"No, no, everything's okay now, thanks," Emma insisted, cutting off her stepmother's offer before it could be made. She turned to her grandmother. "Could I stay with you tonight, Grammy? I don't—I don't . . .''

"I insist on it, dear," Sarah Masterson said. "And tomorrow, Tony will bring you back here for Stan."

Emma smiled and nodded. Then she turned to her father and stepmother. An awkward embrace for him, a perfunctory kiss for her. "Thanks for coming."

"Of course, darling," Mrs. Vale said. "If you need anything—well, your room at the house is always ready."

Emma nodded again. "Thanks. I'll—I'll call you."

"I'm so glad you're all right—you're *both* all right," Walter said. "Is everything okay with the hospital, and the insurance and everything, because—"

"We're fine, really," Emma quickly assured him.

I watched this scene, thinking, Of course she's fine. She has more money than her father . . .

Then Emma turned to Jenny and me. "Thank you for being here. And thank Mr. Lannigan for—for everything."

I nodded as she and Jenny embraced, and then we all

left the hospital. There were two limousines in the parking
lot. Mr. and Mrs. Vale were driven away in one, and Mrs.
Masterson insisted that we all ride with her. A liveried
chauffeur—Tony, I guessed—held the door for us, and then
he drove us back to Manhattan.

It was going on ten o'clock when Mrs. Masterson dropped
us off where I requested, on the corner of Second Avenue
and Sixth Street. We thanked her again, said good night to
her and Emma, and stood watching the limousine glide
away. Then I walked immediately into the block, to the
door beside the bar on the corner. Jenny followed.

There were six buzzers next to the door, two indicating
the second floor. The name beside number 2B was Bernini.
2F—second floor front, I reasoned—was blank. Of course.
I pressed that buzzer. We waited a moment, then I pressed
it again.

"Yeah?" came the voice through the ancient squawk
box.

"Chap, it's Joe Wilder. Jenny's with me. Can we buy
you a cup of coffee?" I was thinking of the place around
the corner, where his friend Amber worked.

He surprised me by buzzing us into his building. We
passed through a tiny foyer with six mailboxes—one of
which bore no nameplate—and up a narrow flight of stairs.
A single naked lightbulb did what it could to illuminate the
dingy gray walls of the second floor landing and the two
plain gray doors on either side of it. It was as cheerless a
place as I had ever seen.

Then the door of apartment 2F opened. Chap stood there,
in jeans and a white T-shirt, clutching a brown beer bottle
in one hand. He looked more serious than usual, which was
very serious indeed. More than serious, I thought: angry.
Without a word, he stepped aside to let us pass, and we
walked into a room that was the true definition of the word
cheerless.

It had once been white, but the walls had faded to some-

thing closer to yellow. One largish room, with the two windows at the front, a kitchenette in a corner near the main
door, and two other doors. Bathroom and closet, probably.
A sheet-covered mattress rested on a box spring below the
windows. A rickety, cigarette-burned table and two wooden
chairs stood near the counter separating the kitchenette
from the main part of the room. A large, dull blue rug
covered the center of the dull wood floor. Two faded art-
works, a framed Picasso print and a long-ago season poster
for Carnegie Hall, hung on the walls.

There were only two gracious touches in the place. One
was a large reclining armchair upholstered in brown leather
near the middle of the room. The other was along the wall
opposite the kitchenette: a big, floor-to-ceiling metal wall
unit of shelves. These were crammed with books, records,
and compact discs, and in the center of the unit was a fairly
new, sleekly designed and obviously expensive music center with turntable, disc player, and AM-FM radio. Four
small speakers, one in each corner of the room, provided
up-to-the-minute surround sound. I glanced at a few of the
titles on the books and discs: classics, both literary and
musical. He'd been reading *Madame Bovary* in the lobby
of Emma's building, claiming that it was because she had
recommended it to him. Now, looking at his collection, I
realized that he'd probably read it before. The man was an
enigma.

He took our coats, hung them in what turned out to be
the closet, and offered us the chairs at the table. We sat.
He asked if we would like coffee or beer, and we declined.
There was an ashtray on the table before me, so I lit a
cigarette. When he was sure we were comfortable, he sat
in the armchair facing us. We all regarded each other for a
long moment. It was Jenny who broke the silence.

"What's wrong, Chap?" she asked.

He looked from her to me, then shrugged and took a pull
from his beer bottle. He swallowed and said, "I don't think
this arrangement is gonna work."

Jenny stared at him. "Why?"

Another shrug. "I fucked up." Another swig of beer.

When it was clear that he didn't intend to elaborate, I said, "How did you fuck up?"

"I didn't get a good look at the car," he said, "and they got away. You asked me to protect her. Some protection, huh?" He shook his head in what I interpreted as self-disgust.

So that was it. I smiled. "Chap, you just saved the lives of two people. I'm the one who's paying you. Do you hear me complaining about your work so far?"

Shrug number three. "I fucked up."

"Stop saying that!" I commanded, surprising myself at the authority in my voice. "You did great, better than I could have done. You're doing fine. You said you protect people. You protected them."

I paused a moment, thinking of my own recent suspicions about the case. It suddenly occurred to me that his real worry was something else, something quite different. I looked at Jenny. No, she didn't get it. I would have to say it, bring it out in the open, and I would have to do it in front of her. Oh, well, so be it.

I locked my gaze with Chap Lannigan's, took a deep breath, and said, "You think she's doing it herself, don't you?"

There was a gasp, a sharp intake of breath from Jenny, who turned to stare at me. I was looking at Chap. In the sudden, odd silence that followed, he slowly lowered his gaze to the bottle in his hand.

"The thought occurred to me," he said. He raised the bottle to his lips and drained it.

Jenny was on her feet in an instant. She stared from him to me, incredulous. "What?! That's insane! What are you talking about?"

One of these days, Chap Lannigan may cease to surprise me, but that day hasn't arrived yet. He looked up at Jenny and said, "Agatha Christie."

I laughed. It was awful: We had just accused one of Jenny's best friends of fraudulent behavior and possible attempted murder. Jenny was quite justifiably outraged. And I was laughing. It welled up inside me, spilling out into the shabby room. Even Chap stared. I couldn't help myself, though. Now that my suspicion had been spoken, I realized just how ridiculous it sounded. With a massive effort, I pulled myself together and made an attempt at damage control.

"Okay," I said, willing the laughter to stop. "Sit down, Jenny."

She surprised me by obeying.

There is an Agatha Christie story—I won't say which one—where one of the heirs to a huge fortune claims that several attempts have been made on their life. Furthermore, one or two people in the heir's immediate orbit have "inadvertently" died as a result. The detective ultimately concludes that the heir—the apparent victim—is actually the villain, systematically knocking off everyone else who shares the fortune. I explained this now to Jenny. Chap listened in silence. He already knew the story.

"But that doesn't make sense," Jenny said when I had finished. "It doesn't apply here. Emma inherited everything, in accordance with her great-grandfather's wishes. She's not sharing it with anyone—she got it all, outright. Besides, the only other person who's been hurt is her husband, who would only get money if *she* were to die. What would be her motive in trying to kill *him*? Unless . . ." She trailed off, thinking.

"Yes," I said, nodding. "Unless *he's* trying to kill *her*. Which might have been the case—until this afternoon. Why hire someone to ram the car in which you're a passenger, a car in which only the driver's side has an airbag? No, if Stan Smith were behind this, he'd have made damn sure that *he* was driving and *she* was in the passenger seat. *He's* the one who was nearly killed, not Emma. It doesn't wash."

We all thought about that for a while. Then Jenny looked from Chap to me and said, "Why did you guys think it might be Emma?"

Chap, that famous conversationalist and raconteur, merely shrugged and looked expectantly at me.

I reached across the scarred wooden table and took her hand in mine. "Go back to the beginning, Jenny. You're at a party, a class reunion in the grand ballroom at the Waldorf-Astoria, of all places. Your old pal, now one of the richest women around, tells you this bizarre thing: 'Somebody's trying to kill me.' When we go to her apartment, she explains it, and the explanation is even more dramatic. The car on the FDR Drive. The switched aspirin. The emergency room at Lenox Hill." I squeezed her hand. "Okay, you're her friend, so you simply accept the whole thing. Well, I'm *not* her friend, and neither is Chap. We don't know this woman from Eve. Think about it: If you didn't know Emma, and you heard this story, what would *you* make of it?"

She pulled her hand away, regarding Chap and me. "Did you two actually discuss this?"

I shook my head. "We didn't have to. It was the obvious explanation. Obvious to everyone—except you. Well, I can't speak for Chap, but I've changed my mind. I don't think it's Emma. In fact, I'm certain of it."

"What made you change your mind?" Jenny asked.

I smiled. "You did. Just now, a few moments ago. You heard our theory, and you were out of that chair like a shot. The look on your face—well, you were ready to defend her to the death. I don't know Emma, but I think I know you." I proceeded carefully here, remembering St. Thomas. "You have never been casual in your affections, and you're no fool. You wouldn't let friendship—or even love—stand in the way of suspicion."

She lowered her gaze to the surface of the table between us, biting her lip. Then, almost imperceptibly, she nodded.

"So, you see, I don't think it's Emma," I said. "Because

you don't. That's good enough for me." I turned to Chap, who'd been watching us closely. "I hope it's good enough for you, too."

He nodded.

"Okay," I said, and we all relaxed. "Chap, you can't blame yourself for anything. There was no way you could have gone after the black car, not with the other cars in the way. Besides, Emma and Stan needed help immediately. You did the right thing, and I don't want to hear any more about it."

He shrugged and nodded again.

"Now," I continued, "Emma talked to the police in the emergency room. I haven't heard from her about it yet—there were too many people around—but I'm willing to bet she spun a yarn. Told them she lost control of the—no. Stan will remember being hit by the other car, and Chap and the other witnesses mentioned it. But she probably said it was an accident, at any rate. She doesn't want the police all over this, which leaves her and the three of us in this room. We're the only ones who know it wasn't an accident. Well, almost—whoever's behind it knows that, too, but we have one advantage over them."

"And what is that?" Jenny asked.

I smiled again. "They—or he, or she—*they* don't know that *we* know."

Another silence descended. I looked around Chap's dreary room, and I couldn't help wondering about him. At that time I knew nothing of his history, his family and his early life. I wondered how much money he had—very little, apparently—and when his last "protection" job had been. I was beginning to like him, and I was glad to be paying him an exorbitant amount of the Mongoose Fund to work with us. I made a mental note then and there: When this was over, when Emma Vale Smith was no longer in danger, I would extend to him the invitation I had already made to Jenny. I would offer him permanent employment.

"So," Jenny said, "what now?"

I laughed again, and this time they both joined me.

"Now," I said, "we proceed to theory number two."

Chap leaned forward in the armchair. "What's theory number two?"

I told them. I talked for a long time. It was nearly midnight when I finished, and through it all they listened intently. I spoke of the past, and of the present, and of the significance of names. Of the slowly forming pattern, the striking similarities between the events of sixteen years ago and today. After a while they both nodded. At last, I thought, the three of us are in agreement.

Then, at midnight, we began to devise a plan of action.

TEN

Sudden Exits

The first week of March is an interesting time to be in New York. It is a time of transition, that interlude between bleak winter and green spring, and the city is in a state of suspended animation. There may be late snow or early rain, but, by and large, it is neither warm nor cold: even the weather is neutral. The trees are still bare, but if you close your eyes and listen, you can almost hear the leaves and new buds pushing outward, straining toward their goals. Everything—streets, skyscrapers, parks, people—seems to be poised on a brink, waiting for something to happen.

Everything but me. On Monday, two days after the incident on the Brooklyn Bridge, I was already in motion. My two new colleagues and I had agreed on pursuing my theory, hazy and unformed as it was, for the simple reason that no one had a better idea. That may not sound particularly scientific, but it can't be helped. We are not scientists.

I had made a list in my mind of things that would have to be done, and I was now on my way to perform the first and most immediate task. Stan Smith had left the hospital the day before, and he and Emma were currently staying at her grandmother's apartment, which was good. But it wasn't good enough. If Walter Vale was telling the truth—and I had no reason to think he wasn't—he would be on his way to Tokyo sometime today. That didn't alter my agenda, and it certainly did nothing to allay my fears. The person or persons behind all this had far-reaching powers. The black sedan that had twice assaulted Emma's car was driven by someone who was essentially an employee. I was certain of that, and I was certain that Emma and her husband were even now in grave danger.

I couldn't do anything at this point to stop the danger, because I wasn't sure who was responsible. Even if I were, I couldn't do anything without proof. This fact had brought the three of us to our course of action. We would remove Emma Vale Smith from harm's way, and then—well, first things first.

I had to wait in the lobby of Sarah Masterson's building on Fifth Avenue while the doorman announced me. I'd expected this because I hadn't called ahead. I was there uninvited. But I was there, and I wasn't leaving until I had accomplished my mission. After several minutes of house phone conversation, the doorman waved me in.

The maid who opened the door took my coat and told me to go into the living room. Emma and Stan were there, but Mrs. Masterson was not.

"Good morning, Joe," Emma said.

She and her husband were wearing bathrobes, and there was a coffee service on the table before them. The maid brought in another cup and saucer and placed it near me as I sat down across from them. There was a bandage on Emma's hand where she had been cut by glass, but it was nothing compared to the gauze-and-tape arrangement on Stan's right temple. The deep blue bruise was visible below the gauze, down that side of his face to the bottom of his ear. Small bandages dotted his neck and hands. More glass cuts, I guessed. But, all in all, he looked considerably better than I'd expected. He'd been lucky—they'd both been lucky. But luck is not something we could count on indefinitely. You really can't count on it at all.

"How are you feeling?" I asked him, just to make sure my impression was correct.

"Oh, I'm okay," he said, grinning. "A little pain up here"—he pointed to his forehead—"but nothing major, thank God. Is your friend Mr. Lannigan around? I'd like to thank him."

So, I thought, she's told him. Good.

"Actually," I said, "that's what I came to talk about. I have a suggestion for the two of you. Just hear me out before you say anything, and then I'll have a cup of coffee while you discuss it. But I must tell you that time is an important factor here, so you're going to have to decide what you want to do before I leave here. Where's Mrs. Masterson?"

"Not here," Emma said. "A bridge luncheon thing, with friends."

"Does she know what's going on?"

"No," they said in unison. Then Emma added, "We decided not to worry her with all this." She waved her hand absently.

I nodded. Then I told them the plan. They sat there on the couch together, listening in silence. At one point, Stan reached over and took his wife's hand in his. When I was finished, I leaned forward to pour myself a cup of coffee. I was just rising to take it and myself away to some other room while they talked it over, when Emma stopped me.

"All right," she said. She looked over at Stan, who nodded. "We'll do as you suggest."

I sank back into my seat.

We sat in silence for a few moments. Then Stan said, "What happens now?"

I smiled to reassure them, not to mention myself.

"Now," I said, "you disappear."

• • •

I left them soon after that and went to Jenny's apartment
in Gramercy Park. There, the two of us ate the lunch she
prepared and waited for news.

It was a good while before we heard anything. Emma
and Stan had listened as I described the whole sequence of
events in which they would soon be involved, but they had
added one detail of their own. They insisted on waiting
until Emma's grandmother returned from her bridge game
and explaining things to her. Though at first reluctant to
involve Mrs. Masterson, they decided that they could not
simply vanish from her home without telling her why. I
agreed to this, but I made one thing very plain: they were
not to tell her—or *anyone*, I stressed—where they were
going.

I didn't like the idea of Emma telling her grandmother
what was happening. It wasn't that I suspected her of being
involved in the plot; I didn't. I just wasn't certain that a
woman of Mrs. Masterson's power and determination
would agree to sit quietly by while everything I'd planned
was going on. If she were to do anything rash—call the
police, or, worse, start questioning family and friends herself—the result could be disastrous. Whoever it was would
be warned, and they would become even more careful than
they'd already been. They might succeed in harming Emma
without being so much as suspected. I couldn't allow that.
I made a mental note to visit Mrs. Masterson this evening
myself, to explain the situation more fully.

While Jenny and I waited for the telephone to ring, I
pictured it all in my mind. Emma and Stan would have
bags, I assumed; small, overnight things that she would
have thrown together and brought with her to her grandmother's apartment. Toothbrushes, makeup, shaving needs,
a couple of changes of clothes. That would keep them comfortable temporarily. Other things could be bought later.

As soon as Sarah Masterson was home and they had
explained it to her, they would go down to the lobby and
ask the doorman to hail them a taxi. This would take them

downtown to a street in the mid-Forties, in the crowded Diamond District. The taxi was to turn left into the street and drop them off at the entrance to an alley halfway between Fifth and Madison.

In the alley, Emma and Stan would get into the backseat of a rental car driven by a man I knew only by his first name, Vito. Vito would drive straight through the alley to the next block and turn right. By this time another car would be following them. If anyone had tailed the Smiths from Mrs. Masterson's building and tried to follow them through the alley, the second car would be ready for them. Chap was in that car, and he was armed. There was a chance this could end today, in an alley in the Diamond District.

I doubted this, and so did Chap. We were certain that no one—good or bad—had any reason to anticipate what Emma and Stan were doing. Until an hour ago, even *they* hadn't anticipated it. I wanted these people to disappear from the face of the earth until further notice, and the element of surprise was on my side.

So, the stocky, muscular, capable-looking man I had briefly met yesterday would drive the Smiths the rest of the way, and Chap would be right behind them. When they reached their destination, Vito would drive away, leaving Chap to take them into their temporary home and get them comfortably settled. Then he would call us.

Another part of the forest: while all this was going on, another of Chap's mysterious associates, a huge African-American man named Jimmy, would be in a third rental car. This car would be waiting a discreet distance from the front gate of the house in Oyster Bay, and—

The telephone rang, interrupting my reverie. I snapped to attention as Jenny picked up the receiver, announced herself, and listened for several moments.

She said, "Yes," and then, "Yes," again. She replaced the phone and looked over at me. "They've arrived. No incidents."

I couldn't help smiling at her. She'd only been doing this for a few days, and already she was picking up the lingo. Well, I *assume* it's the lingo. I'm a stranger here, myself.

After that, we waited some more. I asked her if she had a deck of playing cards. She did, so I spent the next hour teaching her to play five card stud. She spent the hour after that repeatedly beating me. Joe Wilder, cardsharp *extraordinaire*.

Then the phone rang again, and this time I answered it.

It was Jimmy. He had waited a long time before the gates swung open and the Vales' limousine emerged. He followed it from Oyster Bay to Kennedy International, keeping a good distance between himself and the limousine on the Long Island Expressway.

At the airport, the limousine dropped off Walter and Ann Vale and a man who carried Mr. Vale's bags in front of the TWA terminal. They went in, and the chauffeur remained with the car.

Jimmy parked and followed the Vales inside. He watched from a distance as Mr. Vale checked in at the First Class counter. As soon as the bags were checked, the manservant went out to wait in the car with the driver. The Vales went into the cocktail lounge, where they were soon joined by two men and a woman—all white, all middle-aged and well dressed, all bearing airline tickets. When the flight was announced, the Vales kissed and embraced. Then Walter and the three others in the Masterson Electronics party went off to the departure gate, and Mrs. Vale returned to the limousine. Walter Vale was definitely on his way to Japan.

I thanked Jimmy, made sure that he understood and would follow his further instructions, and hung up.

Jenny had disappeared into her bedroom while I was on the phone, and now she emerged in fresh clothes.

"Everything on schedule?" she asked.

I shrugged. "I guess so."

"Good. You and I are going shopping."

"We are?"

"Uh-huh. Food shopping. Then we're going to see Emma and Stan, and I'm making dinner for all of us. If they have to leave their home and spend an indefinite amount of time in a strange place at our request, I think the least we owe them is a home-cooked meal."

"I see," I said. I *did* see: Jenny knew her friend would be feeling fairly disoriented by now. "Okay, let's do that. But first I have to check my answering machine."

She watched me as I picked up her phone and dialed my home number. I smiled at her, deciding that now was not the time to explain that Monday evening was telephone time at my apartment. Donna Crain, my own personal *Malibu Cop*, always called from L.A. at about six o'clock, New York time, three o'clock, her time. We usually spent an hour or two on the phone. It was after six now, and I was wondering if she'd been trying to reach me.

She had. "Hi, babe. Are you there? . . . Guess not. Either that or you're writing something and can't be disturbed." (Sound of giggling.) "I've just spent three hours diving into a swimming pool about a million times, just for one lousy shot! Who says show biz isn't glamorous? Oh, well, I'll try you again later, or *you* can actually pick up the phone and call *me*." (More giggling.) "I'm at the beach house. 'Bye." (Kissing sounds, followed by a click.)

I was about to replace the receiver when a second message began. This one was from my mother.

"Joe, it's me. I just got a call from—umm—oh, damn! I *hate* talking into these things. Just call me when you get this, okay?" (Click.)

I rolled my eyes, which is what I always do when Mom tries to leave a message on my machine. She has no patience with modern technological breakthroughs, and answering machines are a particular bugaboo. I called her immediately.

"Hello?"

"Hi, Mom."

"Joe! Where are you? I've been trying to—"

"I'm at Jenny Hughes's apartment. What's going on?"

"I want you to come here, Joe."

"You mean *now*?"

"*Yes*, I mean now. You've got some explaining to do. Get a cab, you've got twenty minutes."

"Okay, but what—"

"Just get over here." (Click.)

I stared over at Jenny as I replaced the receiver. "I think I'm in trouble."

"What's the matter?" she asked.

I shook my head. "I don't know, but my mom is very upset about something. At the risk of sounding like a ten-year-old, I gotta go home. You get dinner for Emma and Stan, and I'll meet you all as soon as I can."

Jenny shrugged. "Okay. Say hello to your mother for me."

I grabbed my coat, left Jenny's, and hailed a cab. I was at my mother's building on Fifth Avenue in less than the time she'd allotted me.

I mentioned before that my mom's apartment, like Jenny's, resembles a West Indian cottage. Unlike Jenny, Mom has a penthouse, six rooms and a terrace and views in all four directions. She also has animals, a colorful variety of dogs and cats. I can never remember how many she has at any given moment, but they all arrived at the front door the minute I put my key in the lock. I came into the foyer to a symphony of barks, yaps, and meows, and something small and black actually leaped up, dug in, and hung suspended from my pant leg.

"Hello, everybody," I said, automatically beginning to count the poodles and Persians and so forth. I stopped at seven, wondering where Mom was. When I stepped toward the living room, everyone immediately shut up and followed me in eerie silence. This was not a good sign: they usually bark you all the way into the room.

Linda Wilder, when she is standing, is a tall, blond, lovely woman, and her smile is always a welcome sight.

She was not standing at the moment, and she was definitely not smiling. She sat rather rigidly on one of the couches, and she was smoking a cigarette. This is a worse sign than the uncharacteristically quiet animals, because she usually only smokes late at night. Otherwise, it is a certain indicator that she is upset.

When I looked from her to the woman sitting on the other couch, the mystery of my mother's behavior was solved.

It was Sarah Masterson.

Neither woman spoke. They sat there, staring at me. I reached back, pushed two cats off of the chair behind me, sat down, and began to talk.

Twenty minutes later, I had managed to calm them down. And I had managed to do it without really telling them anything. Joe Wilder, politician.

Emma and Stan had told Mrs. Masterson very little. When they left her apartment, they simply said that the car incident was an attempt on Emma's life and that it hadn't been the first. When she'd demanded to know more, they'd told her not to worry, that Joe Wilder was looking into it, and everything was going to be fine. Then they took off, and Sarah Masterson immediately called my mother.

Now I simply repeated what they'd already told her, filling in a few details about the FDR Drive. I didn't mention the aspirin incident, because that would suggest to Sarah Masterson what she did not yet suspect, that Emma's tormentor was probably a friend or family member. I concluded by saying that Emma and Stan had put their trust in me, and that I was indeed looking into it.

When I was finished, Mrs. Masterson regarded me in silence for a long while.

"So," she said at last, never removing her penetrating gaze, "you're looking into this, as you say."

"Yes."

"Do you have any experience with—with this sort of thing?"

"Yes."

"Do you have any idea who may be responsible?"

"Yes."

"But you're not going to tell me?"

"No. Not until I'm certain."

She frowned. "Why don't we just call the police?"

"We can't," I said. "They won't be able to do anything. There's no proof that any crime has been committed—and I have no proof for the theory I'm working on."

She was still frowning. "And when will you have this—proof?"

I met her gaze with my own.

"Give me the rest of the week," I said. "Until Saturday. If I'm no further along, I'll turn it over to you. You can go to the police if you like, but I don't think they'll be able to help you."

She looked from me to my mother. "What do you think, Linda?"

Mom shrugged. Her anger had vanished, replaced by bewilderment. Even the animals surrounding her watched me with suspicion.

"I really don't understand all this," she said. "This is the first I'm hearing of any of it. But I can assure you, Sarah, that my son has had some experience with crime and criminals. I think you should do as he suggests."

I smiled my thanks to her. She nodded.

Sarah Masterson's frank gaze bored into me again. "Joe, is my granddaughter safe?"

I wasn't going to lie to this woman. "She is as safe as she can possibly be—for now."

"What does that mean, 'for now?' "

"She and Stan are in a safe place, and there are people with them. People who will protect them. As long as no one can get to her, she is not in any immediate danger."

We stared some more. This time, Mrs. Masterson was the first to blink.

"Very well," she said. "You have until Saturday—on one condition. You must tell me where Emma is."

"Okay," I conceded, "but only if you promise not to go there. You may be followed."

Her eyes widened, but she didn't ask any more questions. She merely nodded.

I told her where Emma was, and I gave her the phone number there. Then, as I was preparing to leave my mother's apartment and go there myself, Mrs. Masterson said something that changed everything.

"All this secrecy," she said to my mother. "All this running around and hiding. First Craig, now Emma. What on earth has gotten into everybody?"

Now it was my turn to stare. "What do you mean? Where's Craig?"

"I wish I knew!" she said. "My *other* granddaughter is beside herself. No sooner do they announce their engagement than he takes off. She hasn't seen or heard from him since Saturday morning."

I remembered the hospital waiting room Saturday evening. Young Sarah, Sarah Vale, had gone over to the pay phone several times, trying to reach Craig. She hadn't reached him, and now she hadn't seen him in three days. Ever since—

That's it, I thought. That's the connection. Sixteen years ago and the present.

I excused myself, went into my mother's office, and picked up the telephone.

ELEVEN

Leg Work, Part One

I have this thing about flying.

I wasn't always so nervous, of course. I grew up in St. Thomas, and there's only one way on or off the island, barring a slow boat. Planes are hardly the novelty for me that they are for most people. If you throw in several trips to Europe, I can honestly say that I've been on just about everything that flies, from the Concorde to those rickety, amphibious, five-seat "island hoppers." I've flown more than most, and I used to love it.

Not anymore, though. I am thirty-seven as I write this, nearly forty, and I differ from the child and the young man who looked forward to plane trips in one major way: I have recently accepted the fact of my mortality. I am not invincible, and planes—to put it quite simply—crash.

When I try to explain my feelings to people, they smile indulgently and rattle off a lot of helpful statistics which prove that flying is by far the safest form of transportation. I nod my head sheepishly and tell them that, whereas I understand and appreciate that I'm far more likely to be killed in the cab on the way to the airport than in the plane, the simple truth of the matter is that I'd rather take my chances in the cab. I am not a coward, and I don't think I particularly fear death. Still, I prefer to face it on the ground than in a tiny silver cylinder miles above the earth, thank you very much.

When the seat belt sign came on and the flight attendant announced that we were entering our final approach, I put down the paperback thriller I'd been trying to concentrate on for two hours and dug my fingers into the armrests. The bored, frequent-flier businessman in the First Class seat beside me smiled at my obvious distress, patted my hand, and rattled off the taxi/plane statistic. I grimaced a smile at him before closing my eyes, remembering another statistic: ninety-five percent of all air disasters occur during takeoffs and landings.

We were destined not to become a statistic today. With a couple of gentle thumps and a roar of locking, perfectly functional landing gear, the Delta 747 glided smoothly down the sunlit runway. Minutes later, having opened my eyes and willed myself to stop shaking, I walked off the plane into the carpeted passageway that led to the terminal at Tampa International Airport.

It is a very attractive city. I've been in various places in Florida at various times, but I'd never been here before. I'd never been on Florida's west coast, which doesn't look anything like its east coast. The water in the Gulf of Mexico, which provides the town with its dazzling waterfront, is a richer, deeper blue than the Atlantic, or so it appeared to me when I first saw it from my balcony at the hotel. And the green that is everywhere—grass, foliage, stately palm trees—seems darker than elsewhere. The colors are definitely more subdued than in St. Thomas.

But what I really hadn't expected was the nature of the city itself. The highway from the airport, the wide streets and avenues, the ultramodern skyscrapers, the festive market squares near the harbor: it was clear to see why this is one of the fastest-growing cities in America. Everything is clean and well tended, and the natives are an attractive, friendly lot. Naturally, the weather is lovely—I had come from gray New York in the forties to this sunny, verdant place with a temperature in the low seventies—but the magic is something more. I stared around at the buildings and the boats and the smiling, well-dressed people, thinking that I had rarely seen anywhere so *upscale*. That was the word that came to my mind, and it was appropriate.

Of course, growing up in a tourist resort had taught me the biggest rule of vacation towns: the tourists see exactly what the natives want them to see. Even this beautiful city has its downside, as I was soon to discover.

There was a basket of fruit on the bureau of my fifth-floor room in the hotel, and the card inside read Welcome to Tampa. Yes, I thought automatically, they do that in St. Thomas, too, only there you get mangoes and pineapples. The star of this cornucopia was the famous Florida orange, as well it should be.

I took a quick shower and put on a fresh shirt under my lightweight suit. Then I had a sandwich in one of the restaurants in the lobby—I couldn't eat in the plane—and went out to the taxi stand. I gazed longingly down toward the bay for exactly five seconds before reminding myself that I was not a tourist, not here on vacation. I had a job to do.

The Yellow Cab looked surprisingly like those we have in New York, but there the similarity ended. The driver was a burly, friendly, middle-aged man for whom English was a first language. He, like the fruit basket, welcomed me to Tampa. When I read the address on the scrap of my mother's notepaper where I'd jotted it the night before, his smile disappeared.

"Are you sure of that address, sir?" he asked. "Are you *sure* that's where you want to go?"

I repeated what I'd written. With a shrug of resignation, he pulled out into the midday traffic. In minutes he'd transferred to a highway that seemed, though I wasn't familiar

with the layout, to be taking me away from the city itself.
The bay and the skyscrapers disappeared, replaced by well-
appointed homes in pretty neighborhoods. Then came what
I guessed was an affluent suburb; big houses on wide, well-
tended lawns. Still we continued on.

Real estate decreases in value the farther you get from
water. It will suffice to say that the neighborhood—or,
more likely, adjacent town—to which I was driven that
afternoon was definitely *inland*. At first, I didn't notice the
dramatic change in the landscape. I was replaying in my
mind the odd phone conversation of the night before.

It was remarkably easy to locate her. I simply called Tampa
information, which provided me with an address and phone
number in a matter of seconds. I dialed the number, which
was answered on the third ring.

"'Lo?" A slurred female voice, oldish, distinct southern
accent.

"Mrs. Dolores Trent, please," I said.

"You got her."

"Hello, Mrs. Trent. My name is Joe Wilder. I'm a journalist here in New York, and I'm doing a story on famous
crimes in the Long Island area. I was wondering if you'd
be willing to—"

"Famous crimes, you say?" Harsh, suspicious.

"Yes, that's right. I'm referring to—"

"Oh, Judas Priest Almighty, I *know* what you're 'referring to,' Mr. New York Journalist. How much?"

"I beg your pardon?"

"He begs my pardon! My pardon ain't been begged in
a dog's age! How *much*, Mr.—what the hell was it again?"

"Wilder. Joe Wilder."

"Joe Wilder. Sounds like a comic strip. The New Adventures of Joe Wilder, Boy Astronaut." She broke off
here, cackling at her own joke. At last the fit was controlled
and the slurred voice continued. "So, Mr. Astronaut, you
want to talk to me about Mike and that Mrs. Vale, right?

Are you with the *New York Times*, or somethin'?''

"Uh, no, I'm with—a magazine. *New York* magazine."
Six months to a year for misrepresentation, I thought, and
all the *café latté* and balsamic vinegar you can carry.

"Well, then, you just tell me how much *New York* magazine is gonna pay me to talk to you for this article on
famous Long Island crimes, Mr. Joe Wilder."

I was in uncharted waters here. "Five hundred dollars?"

Dead silence. Then:

"No shit!"

"No—um, that's correct."

"Well, fire away!"

"Excuse me?"

"Ask your questions, Mr. Wilder. I've got all night!"
More cackling.

"Actually, I was wondering if I could interview you in
person."

"You mean, come *here*?"

"If that's all right with you."

"Are you in Tampa, Mr. Wilder?"

"I will be, tomorrow afternoon."

There was another pause. I half-expected her to hang up.
She didn't. "Okay, three o'clock tomorrow afternoon.
You got my address?"

"Yes." I repeated it to her, just to be sure.

"That's it. See you tomorrow—and, Mr. Wilder?"

"Yes?"

"Could you pay me in cash? I got some—uh, some bills
to pay."

"I'll have the money with me. Good-bye."

The cab came to a stop. I blinked and looked around me,
thinking, I'm not in Kansas anymore. I certainly wasn't in
Tampa, at least any part of it where I'd want to be.

It was a white house, one in a long row of little white
houses that didn't look very sturdy and were virtually in-
distinguishable from each other. Each looked to have

maybe four rooms, with identical little front porches, and
open-air carports at the sides. The front lawns were not
really lawns at all, merely tracts of dry dirt, ten feet by
twenty, that had probably never contained grass. A sidewalk ran the length of the street, with identical walkways
leading through the dirt tracts up to each front door. In lieu
of trees there were clotheslines, those rotating metal affairs
set up on central poles that always remind me of the Gug-
genheim Museum, don't ask me why. Sheets and towels
flapped in the breeze beside most of the houses I could see.
The sun glared down on it all, unrelieved by any form of
shade. From somewhere unseen I could hear radio music
and the occasional shouts of children. A thin yellow dog
of indeterminate breed poked around the lidless metal gar-
bage can beside the cab.

The driver was staring at the house. "You want me to
wait?"

"I may be an hour or so," I said. "Do you mind waiting
that long?"

"Nah, I'll leave the meter running." He picked up a
paperback novel from the seat beside him and lit a cigarette.

I nodded, grabbed the airline bag I'd brought with me,
and got out.

Dolores Trent was waiting in her doorway as I came up
the walk. She was an overweight woman somewhere in
her sixties. Gray strands peered through the brown dye job
in her hair, which she wore in an inappropriate, girlish
style, a shoulder-length flip with bangs cascading down
into her rather meaty, overpainted face. She was wearing,
inevitably, shocking blue stretch pants, matching high
heels, and an off-the-shoulder, embroidered Mexican peas-
ant blouse that may look lovely on Mexican peasants but
did nothing for Dolores Trent. Pink coral earrings and
necklace dangled from her ears and ample bosom, and a
cigarette dangled from her scarlet lips. Sarah Masterson's
generation would have referred to this woman as a slattern,
but mine would simply call her a pig.

She squinted up at me through false eyelashes as I arrived at the door.

"Mr. Wilder," she said around the cigarette.

"Mrs. Trent," I said, smiling.

She smiled, too. "Call me Dolly. Everybody does."

I wondered who "everybody" was as she turned around and led me into her living room. Three distinct odors assaulted me simultaneously: stale smoke, lemon-scented air freshener, and Mrs. Trent's cloying perfume. The house itself was reasonably well furnished and surprisingly clean. I remembered that she was, or had been, a nurse. I guess some habits die hard.

I reevaluated her as she seated me in the easy chair across the coffee table from the couch and went into the kitchen for her "special" lemonade. I knew I was being a snob: she wasn't a pig, merely a lower-middle-class ex-nurse of limited means and education, a divorcée who had presumably done her best to raise the handsome son whose face smiled out from several framed photographs on a nearby table. She'd already lost her husband when she lost her son to tragedy.

It was of that tragedy that she immediately began to speak when she came back with a pitcher of lemonade and two glasses. I'd taken a cassette player from the airline bag and placed it on the table. She sat on the couch and poured as I started the recorder.

"I don't know why you folks would be interested in Mike, especially now," she said. "I've spent sixteen years trying to live it down. I was a nurse for thirty years, you know. A good nurse, too. Finally made it onto the administrative staff. Nearly a hundred people under me, I had. But that didn't matter, what *I* did, what *I* accomplished. Everybody just wanted to know about Mike. Mike and that woman. Mike this, Mike that. That's what it does to you, you know, to your life. For sixteen years I've been Michael Trent's Mother. Period." She shrugged, took a sip of her "special" lemonade, and lit a fresh cigarette.

I took a sip, too, and nearly choked. What made it "special" was the gin.

"Mrs. Trent—Dolly, I know all about the incidents in New York, and I know all about Laura Vale. I was hoping you could tell me about your son before that, before he left Tampa."

"Just like his father," she said at once. "*Exactly*! I loved the both of 'em somethin' fierce, not that it did me any good. Bob Trent was a construction foreman. Biggest, handsomest man you ever saw. He got hurt putting up one of those big buildings downtown, fell off a scaffold and broke an arm and a leg. That's how we met, at the hospital. I took one look at him and—well, he was unconscious at the time. I didn't see him drinking and womanizing, which is how he spent most of his time when he was awake. So I married the sonofabitch.

"Mike came along, and he took right after his daddy. Looked like him, too—the both of 'em too handsome for their own good. Fifteen, sixteen years old, and Mike was already out with the boys and off with the women. I can't even blame his daddy, 'cause I'd thrown *him* out when Mike was still in diapers. It must be some genetic thing." She eyed me with suspicion, and I could tell that she had long ago dismissed my entire gender as womanizing drunks.

I nodded in what I hoped was a sympathetic, nonwomanizing, nonalcoholic fashion. "So, did he get in a lot of trouble?"

She laughed, the cackle I'd first heard on the phone the night before. "Honey, he was never *out* of it! Never finished high school. Dropped out, not that it mattered—they were about to expel him, anyway. I knew he was probably doing drugs, you know, cocaine, and it turned out I was right. And one time him and a couple of his friends trashed a bar over in St. Pete, but they didn't get caught, more's the pity. Then there was that week he spent in jail for nearly killing a guy—"

"Yes," I said quickly. "Tell me about that. They were lifeguards, I believe."

"That they were. The one thing Mike *could* do, just like his daddy. Swam like a fish, always. So, him and a couple of his pals trained as lifeguards. Worked around on the public beaches, Davis and Bradington, until that last job. Fancy hotel on Harbour Island, the Wyndham. Big fight, right next to the pool. The other guy was one of his best friends, if you can believe it. Over a woman, natch, some rich guest at the hotel they'd both been puttin' it to. Rod ended up in the hospital, and Mike was thrown in jail."

I glanced down at the cassette recorder. It was getting every word. "What was Rod's last name?"

"Hutchinson. Rod Hutchinson. Another good-for-nothin' pretty boy. World's full of 'em—Tampa, at any rate."

Yes, I thought. And New York City . . .

"Do you know where Rod Hutchinson is now?" I asked.

She blinked. "Why do you want to know about *him*? I thought you were doing a story about Mike and Laura Vale."

"I am," I said quickly, reaching into the airline bag and pulling out the rubber-banded stack of twenty dollar bills. "I was just curious."

"He and his brother have a charter boat service over by Rocky Point, last I heard. Sunshine Charters."

I nodded. "How long after the fight did Mike leave Tampa?"

"A few days." She drained her glass and lit another cigarette. "He was in jail for a week. When he got out, he came home here, but he didn't stay. Disappeared for a couple of days, then came back. He packed up his clothes, told me he was gettin' out of town for a while. He was supposed to do this community service, you know, after the jail time. I thought he just didn't want to do it, so he was skippin'. He said he'd call me when he got settled somewhere. Then he took off. A friend of mine, a nurse I worked with, said

she saw him at the airport. He was with a woman, gettin'
on a plane to New York.''

I leaned forward. ''What woman?''

She shrugged. ''Damned if I know. Some woman. Anyway, he called me from New York a couple of times during
the next year. Said he had a lifeguard job there, and that
he'd come back to see me soon. But he never did. I didn't
see him again until—''

She stopped abruptly, staring over at the framed photographs. She took a long drag on her cigarette and poured
herself another glass of lemonade-flavored gin. When she
raised her head, I was surprised to see that her eyes were
wet with tears.

I stood up immediately. I placed the money on the table
and picked up the cassette player.

''Well, thank you for your time, Dolly,'' I said. ''I appreciate it. I'm sorry if this has upset you.''

Dolores Trent ran the back of a hand over her eyes. Remarkably, the false eyelashes remained in place.

'' 'S'okay,'' she said, forcing a smile. ''I ain't upset,
really. He was a bum, just like his daddy. Why the hell
should I cry for him now?''

Because you loved him, I thought, but I didn't say it.

When I returned to the hotel, I asked at the front desk for
a local telephone directory. I found the listing, wrote down
the number, and went up to my room to place the call.

''Sunshine Charters.'' A young woman's voice, friendly,
animated.

''Rod Hutchinson, please,'' I said.

He wasn't there, the woman told me, but he would be in
tomorrow morning at nine. I thanked her and hung up. Then
I called Delta Airlines and confirmed my return flight at
noon. I also called Jenny to check on things there. Everything was fine, she assured me, meaning Emma and Stan.
I told her I'd see her tomorrow. I had an excellent dinner
in one of the hotel's restaurants and went to bed.

The next morning was as warm and sunny as the previous day. I checked out of the hotel shortly after nine o'clock, and another Yellow Cab took me to a marina uptown, near Rocky Point. I asked the driver to wait.

It took several minutes of searching before I found the little wooden shanty with the garishly painted sign, SUNSHINE CHARTERS. The perky young woman at the desk in the shack directed me to a medium-sized Cris-craft, the *Sunshine*, that was tied a few yards away down the dock. As I approached the vessel, I saw two large men in jams and tank tops bending over the open hatch to an inboard motor. One was doing something with a wrench while the other watched.

"Ahoy, *Sunshine*," I called.

The two men straightened and turned around. Big, handsome, fortyish sailors, with sun-streaked blond hair and beards. Brothers, obviously.

"Good morning," the one with the wrench said. "What can we do for you?"

"I'm looking for Rod Hutchinson," I said.

The other man, the slightly younger of the two, leaped up onto the dock beside me. "I'm Rod."

"Joe Wilder," I said, and we shook hands. The brother went back to repairing the motor.

He was forty now, and still very handsome: I could just imagine how he must have looked at twenty-four. I told him what I'd told Dolores Trent, that I was doing a piece on the murder/suicide for *New York*. He stared, curious, and said sure, he'd answer a few questions. He didn't ask for money, and I didn't offer it.

"How's Dolly doing these days?" he asked when I told him about yesterday. "I haven't seen her since—well, since before Mike died."

"She's okay," I said. "She told me you and Mike were friends, and that you got into a fight that landed him in jail."

Rod Hutchinson threw back his head and laughed.

"Yeah," he said, "I *guess* you could call it a fight. More like a slaughter. I didn't get in a single punch, but he damn near killed me."

"You don't seem too upset about it now," I observed. "If it was so funny, why did you press charges?"

"I didn't," he said. "The hotel did. On behalf of their guest, the gal we were arguing about."

"Why were you arguing?"

He laughed again. "Oh, she was something! Gorgeous. Rich. Classy, you know? We were both carrying on with her. She was here recovering from a divorce, she said. She was at the pool every day for a week, lounging around in these tiny bikinis and making eyes at us. We were the life-guards there. So we got to talking to her, flirting, and we both ended up in her room. Not at the same time, of course. I didn't know about him, and he didn't know about me. Until that day. She called us both over and asked which one of us wanted to go to New York with her, all expenses paid. Just like that: she was laughing when she said it, watching us. Well, Mike always had a real temper. When he found out I'd been with her, too, he just lit into me. Broke my nose and two ribs before the security guys arrived to pull him off me. And she just sat there on the lounge chair through the whole thing, laughing her ass off."

I nodded. "And Mike was arrested."

"Yeah," Rod said. "Disturbing the peace on private property, or whatever. He spent a few days in jail, but he was rewarded for it, I guess."

"What do you mean?"

He stared. "I thought you'd know; I figured Dolly must have told you that part. Our mutual girlfriend took him to New York with her. Last I ever saw of him. A year later, I picked up the newspaper and—well, you know the rest."

"Yes," I said. "I know the rest. This woman, the one who took him away with her—was it Laura Vale?"

Rod stared at me again, clearly surprised at the suggestion. "Hell, no, it wasn't her. It was just some rich tourist. She didn't keep him for long up there, apparently. He went to work at a beach club on Long Island, according to the papers. *That's* where he met Laura Vale. Our gal must have thrown him over."

"I see," I said, but I didn't. Not yet, anyway. "Do you remember the woman's name? The tourist woman?"

He thought a moment. He reached up and scratched his beard.

"Mary," he said at last. "Marian. Marilyn. Something like that. I really don't remember. It was all so long ago."

"Thank you, Rod," I said, and I turned to leave.

"So long ago," Rod repeated. I turned back to him. "He was my best friend, you know? We grew up together. I thought I really knew him, but I obviously didn't. He beat the shit out of me and ran off with Marie—*that* was her name, Marie. A year later he killed that woman, Laura Vale, and then he offed himself." He shook his head in bewilderment. "God, I *still* don't believe it!"

I looked at him, at his handsome, bewildered face. Then I looked out at the other boats in the marina, at the bridges shimmering in the distance, at the deep blue water of Tampa Bay. I was remembering my conversation with Emma nearly two weeks before.

"Tell me about Sarah."

"Grammy?"

"No, I mean your sister, Sarah Vale."

"Oh. Her. Two women: one name. And they couldn't be more different if they tried . . ."

"No," I told Rod Hutchinson. "I don't believe it, either."

I left him on the dock and walked back to the waiting cab.

TWELVE

Leg Work, Part Two

I didn't get back to my apartment until five o'clock that afternoon, so I had to put off my next plans until the following day, Thursday. I regretted this, because I was acutely aware of time passing. I had developed a sort of inner clock, some device in my mind and my nervous system, that recorded the hours and minutes, even down to seconds. Throughout my trip to Tampa and the days that followed, I could almost hear it ticking away, like the clock in the crocodile in *Peter Pan*. And as the time went by, diminished, I began to feel as anxious as Captain Hook. Sarah Masterson had given me until Saturday, and only two full days remained. *Tick-tock, tick-tock . . .*

I actually accomplished quite a lot that Wednesday evening. I see that, looking back, but I wasn't aware of it then. Isn't that always the way with memory?

There were two specific things I intended to do the next day, but I wanted to talk to Emma first. I toyed with the idea of calling Sarah Masterson, or even Sarah Vale. As it turned out, I'm glad I didn't. Emma was definitely the right person to approach.

So, Wednesday evening I went to the "hideout," as I

was beginning to think of it. Amber O'Day, the beautiful, red-haired aspiring actress who was Chap's current love interest, lived in a big, two bedroom railroad apartment on East Tenth Street near Second Avenue. It was convenient for her because it was just two blocks north of the coffee-house where she worked, where Jenny and I had first met her. It was convenient for us because she was between roommates. The most recent one, a dancer, had moved out just two weeks before, leaving one bedroom temporarily empty. Emma and Stan were now ensconced in that bed-room, and I was paying for it. More precisely, my absent friend who had left me all his money was paying for it. Amber, if no one else, was delighted with the arrangement.

Jenny and Chap were already there when I arrived at seven o'clock that evening. Moments later, dinner arrived at the door in the form of two pizzas, two pasta dishes, and salad from John's, a local Greenwich Village parlor of in-ternational repute. I tried to intervene when Chap paid the delivery man, but he shook his head and reassured me with one word, whispered under his breath so the others couldn't hear him.

"Mongoose."

So. I—or, rather, my friend—was paying for dinner, af-ter all. I nodded and put my wallet back in my pocket.

I remember that evening fondly now. The five of us sat around the little living room, stuffing ourselves with ex-cellent Italian food and washing it down with soft drinks, which we drank from paper cups. Amber soon joined us, and later the six of us played Trivial Pursuit. We laughed a great deal, and Emma and her husband were more relaxed than I had ever seen them.

I also managed to accomplish what I had gone there to do. At one point in the festivities, after the meal and before the game, the others were spooning out ice cream and mak-ing coffee, and I was able to get Emma aside for a few moments. Keeping my voice low, I asked her two ques-tions.

Her answer to my first question was yes.

She said she did not know the answer to my second question.

When she immediately began to ask questions of her own, I politely but firmly cut her off. I smiled at her and squeezed her hand, and then I went to help Amber set up the game board.

It was a pleasant evening—all the more so because it was the last such evening any of us would have for a long time. Hindsight again. The things we remember, the little things, like pizza and ice cream and Trivial Pursuit . . .

At eleven o'clock the next morning, I was at the wheel of the rental car that Chap had retrieved from the mysterious Vito, the man who had driven Emma and Stan from the alley in the Diamond District to Amber's building two days before. I drove east in the thirties and through the Midtown Tunnel. I paid the toll for the Expressway, then took the first exit after the tollbooth into Long Island City. Consulting the instructions I'd scrawled earlier that morning, I drove three blocks north and pulled into a medium-sized car dealership.

It was part of a chain, one of many in the Northeast, but it was the only Davis dealership in New York City. A recorded voice at the toll-free number listed in the Yellow Pages advertisement had informed me that there was this one in Long Island City, one in Suffolk County, three in various other parts of New York state, two in New Jersey, and three in Connecticut. That was it for the tri-state area. Sherlock Holmes would have tried here first, which is exactly what I was doing. Great minds think alike, you know.

There was a one-story, glass-walled office/showroom in the center of the complex, surrounded on all four sides by parking lots full of big, shiny cars. The lot itself stood alone on a tree-lined block across the street from a busy shopping center. I glanced over there as I got out of the car. A department store, a supermarket, an eight-plex movie theater, various small stores and restaurants. The usual.

This particular Davis dealership was doing fairly good business today, as far as I could tell. Two men in the distinctive, muted maroon blazers and striped ties that were the agency's uniform were showing prospective buyers the latest models of large, expensive American automobiles. Glass and chrome glinted in the sunlight as doors were opened and engines started in preparation for test drives. A third salesperson was enumerating the luxuries of a beautiful Cadillac in the showroom as I came through the glass doors. The heating system inside was working very well, so I unbuttoned my coat as I went over to the main desk.

Two young women in maroon blazers were there, one of them talking into a phone headset. The other, a pretty blond girl with green eyes, smiled and greeted me.

"Good morning," I said. "I'd like to speak with the proprietor, Mr. Jacobs."

She continued to smile. "Do you have an appointment, sir?"

"Uh, no. This is a personal matter."

"Your name?"

"Joseph Wilder. I'm a—a friend of Craig Davis."

"Oh, yes. Craig. One moment, please." She pushed a button on the desk before her and spoke into her headset.

So. She obviously knew Craig Davis. It was a good guess that the proprietor did, as well. Lucky me.

I went over to look at a handsome, dark gray Lincoln Continental while the young woman carried on a rather lengthy, murmured conversation. I glanced at the price sticker on the driver's window. Not bad, I supposed, if you simply *had* to have a means of transportation that costs more than most people's homes. I live in New York, so I no longer own a car. The first thing I did upon moving here from college on Long Island was sell my Honda Civic. Keeping a car in Manhattan means a twenty-four-hour garage. For what it costs, you might as well give up your apartment and sleep in the car. I stared at the gray Lincoln, wondering who—other than the Masterson/Vales—could afford *any* car in New York, let alone this one.

"Mr. Wilder."

I turned back to the desk. The blond girl was still smiling. Employee of the Month, no doubt. She waved me toward a door behind her and pushed a button on the desk that discreetly unlocked it. I smiled and thanked her as I passed.

The inner office was small and cramped, with four windowless walls and floor-to-ceiling shelves and filing cabinets. The shelves were crammed with hundreds of auto catalogs, brochures, and manuals. The walls were covered with car posters, framed photos of cars, and licenses and citations from manufacturers, auto clubs, and various trade groups. The big, framed sheepskin on the wall behind the desk was from the New York Chamber of Commerce. This was an extremely legitimate business—a good thing to know when you're about to ask its proprietor, a complete stranger, several questions he isn't required to answer.

That proprietor, who rose from behind the desk as I came in, was apparently vying with his own employees for Employee of the Month. His smile was brighter, as were his maroon jacket and striped tie. A big man, somewhat overweight, with small features in a big, florid face and short, wiry salt-and-pepper hair. In his early sixties, I guessed.

"Mr. Wilder," he said brightly as he came around the desk and vigorously shook my hand. "I'm Arnold Jacobs. What can I do for you, sir? Any friend of the Davises . . ." He trailed off, his smile freezing and fading when he saw the expression on my face.

It was a stern expression, learned in college acting classes, and my voice matched it.

"Mr. Jacobs," I said, looking directly into his eyes, "I'm not a friend of Craig Davis, or anyone in his family. I'm representing his fiancée, Sarah Vale. I'd like to ask you some questions. It won't take long, just a few moments."

Arnold Jacobs stared. "You're—a detective . . . ?"

I continued to watch him, carefully not answering his question. I was remembering the old Sunday school lesson about the lies of omission crying as loudly to Heaven as the ones we speak. From magazine journalist to licensed private investigator: two false professions in as many days. My feet were getting warm. Add to this the fact that, if my guess about this place was wrong, Mr. Jacobs was going to think I was insane.

After a long, uncomfortably quiet moment, he asked, "Is Craig in some kind of trouble, Mr. Wilder?"

I made a great display of glancing quickly over at the closed door before leaning toward him and lowering my voice. "How well do you know Craig, Mr. Jacobs?"

He blinked, clearly bewildered. And something else: worried. Definitely worried.

"I've known the Davis family since I started this franchise," he said. "Twenty-eight years ago. I've known Craig since he was a little boy. Mr. Wilder, what is this—"

I held up a hand, silencing him.

"Mr. Jacobs," I said, switching immediately from tough detective to man of the world, "I think Craig has got himself in a bit of—trouble." I paused dramatically, going from just any old man of the world to Maurice Chevalier in *Gigi*. "You know, *woman* trouble. Ms. Vale has reason to believe he's seeing another woman."

Understanding dawned on Arnold Jacobs's face. He didn't look terribly surprised at the notion. "Ohhh, *I* get it! And his fiancée has hired you to—"

"I've been following him around lately," I said, cutting him off. I smiled now, increasing the volume from Maurice Chevalier to Anthony Quinn in *Zorba the Greek*. "Last Saturday I saw him and—the woman in question. They were getting into a car—a Lincoln, I believe, from this lot." I continued to smile at him, holding my breath, waiting for the denial that would destroy my house of cards.

There was no denial. Instead, he immediately turned bright red.

"I *knew* it!" he muttered. "I *knew* I shouldn't have lent him the Town Car! Oh, boy. Does—does Sarah Vale know about—"

"Oh, no," I said mildly, cutting him off. Bouzouki music played in my head as I began to dance. "Listen, Mr. Jacobs, I'll be frank with you. Ms. Vale seems like a nice woman, and I must say Mr. Davis seems like a nice man. I haven't told her anything yet, because I don't think this other relationship is serious. But Craig apparently borrowed the car from you to take out this other woman." I gave him a humorously reproachful look, the way Quinn looked at Alan Bates. "Now, it would be a shame if anything screwed up their impending wedding, don't you think?"

"Absolutely!" he said. "What can I do to help?"

"Well," I said, shrugging, "the truth is, I've lost Craig Davis. I can't find him. I haven't seen him since Saturday. Do you know where he is?"

He shook his head. "No, I don't. He just showed up here Friday and asked if he could borrow the car again."

"Again?"

Now he nodded. "Yeah, *again.* He's always doing things like that, borrowing a car or borrowing money. Uncle Arnie, that's what he calls me. He's like a favorite nephew, you know? I feel sorry for him, really, ever since Jack Davis threw him out. I guess you know he's been disinherited. But I didn't know he was using my cars to—well, maybe marriage will straighten him out. You don't—you don't *have* to tell Sarah Vale about the other gal, do you, Mr. Wilder?"

I smiled sympathetically, the worldly Greek who is the friend of young lovers everywhere.

"Maybe not," I said, adding, "not if *you* can help me."

Mr. Jacobs brightened again. "Sure! Anything!"

I felt terrible. I could see he was genuinely fond of Craig, the wayward son of the man who was pretty much his employer. And I was beginning to realize that his fondness was definitely misplaced.

"I haven't been able to identify this other woman," I said. "Do you know her name?"

His eagerness faded. "Gosh, no. I know Craig is engaged to Sarah Vale, and I know he used to see her sister. But until you told me a few minutes ago, I had no idea there was someone else. Of course, he always used to have lots of girls—but not lately. I thought he was serious this time."

"I see," I said, careful not to indicate my disappointment. "Okay. I think I should just have a little talk with him when he shows up." There was a pen on his desk, and a large, block-shaped note pad lay near it. I wrote my name and home number on the pad. "Would you have him call me when he returns the car to you?"

He blinked. "What do you mean?"

I looked at him, at the confusion on his face, not understanding. "You said he borrowed the car on Friday—"

"Yeah, but he returned it."

It was my turn to blink. "He *returned* it?"

"Sure."

"When?" I asked.

Mr. Jacobs opened his mouth to speak, then snapped it shut. A look of puzzlement crossed his face. He opened the door and went out into the showroom. I followed.

"Mindy," he said to the smiling blond girl, "when did Craig Davis return the Town Car he borrowed?" As he said this, he jerked his thumb toward the side lot beyond the glass.

I looked in the direction he'd indicated. There was a single row of cars parked at the edge of the lot, shaded by the trees on the other side of the fence. Five big, shiny Lincoln Town Cars. Only one of them was black.

If Mindy found his question odd, she gave no indication. She thought a moment.

"Monday," she said. "Well, what I mean is, it was here Monday morning when we opened. It was parked on the street outside the gate. Manny couldn't move it at first, because the car was locked and nobody knew where the keys were. I found them when I went to get the mail." She pointed to a white box attached to the outside of the fence near the gates at the front entrance to the lot. "Craig dropped the keys in the mailbox."

"Thank you," Mr. Jacobs said. Then he turned to me. "So, he left the car outside the gate sometime between seven o'clock Saturday, closing time, and eight o'clock Monday morning, when we opened. We're closed on Sunday." He shrugged. "That's the best I can do."

"Has he ever done that before?" I asked.

"What?"

"Left the borrowed car outside the gate."

"No, never," he said. "He always brings me the keys and makes a big deal about thanking me."

"But not this time?"

"No, not this time."

"Okay," I said. I lowered my voice and leaned toward him again, making sure Mindy and her coworker behind the counter couldn't hear me. "One more thing. You said he borrowed a black Town Car *again*."

He looked wary now. "Yes."

"So he's borrowed black Town Cars before?"

"Yes, but—"

"Did he borrow one from you one Monday, about—" I calculated "—six weeks ago?"

Mr. Jacobs stared. "Yes, he did. Mr. Wilder, just how long have you been watching Craig?"

I smiled again. "Long enough. Thank you for your help, Mr. Jacobs. Just call me if you hear from him, okay? I think we can, you know, get him back on track." I actually winked at him and patted him on the shoulder. Two men of the world, protecting one of our own. All boys together.

"Good," said Mr. Jacobs, who winked right back. "*I'm* going to have a little talk with him, too. Now that he's engaged, he's going to have to keep it in his trousers—*hard* as it may be!"

We chuckled together at his incredibly clever, *homme du*

monde witticism, and then he shook my hand and, still chuckling, went back into his office.

I smiled again at the ever-smiling Mindy and went out of the warm showroom into the chilly parking lot.

I felt sick.

I took a few steps in the direction of my car and stopped, looking around as nonchalantly as possible. When I was certain that no one in a maroon blazer was watching me, I ambled over to the row of parked Town Cars.

The black one in the middle stood gleaming before me now. A big, powerful four-door sedan with—

The bile rose in my throat.

—tinted windows.

Emma. The FDR Drive, six weeks ago.

"I remember looking over at the tinted windows: I couldn't see a thing, just the glint of the sunlight."

It took me a mere few seconds to reinforce what I had already guessed. I wasn't even particularly surprised to see the slight nick and the scratch marks on the otherwise pristine black rubber on the right edge of the front bumper, or the small but definite dent in the chrome beside it. This was indeed the mysterious black vehicle that had sent Emma's car crashing into the wall on Saturday afternoon. Not that I'd doubted it.

I ambled ever-so-casually back over to my car, got in, and drove quickly out of the lot, gulping in fresh, freezing air to fight the sudden nausea. The reflection of the big white letters on the rotating maroon sign—DAVIS—remained in my rearview mirror until I turned onto the ramp to the Expressway and headed east toward Long Island.

One hour later, I was standing on a quiet little road near Oyster Bay, looking up at the black wrought-iron gates of the Masterson/Vale estate. My rental car was parked beside the road a hundred yards away. The big yellow house stood in the distance beyond the gates, at the end of a long, tree-lined drive. High stone walls extended into the distance from both sides of the gates. They surrounded the entire complex.

I looked up and down the road. It was basically a large drive that ran parallel to the Sound for about half a mile, with occasional gated turnoffs leading on one side to three or four big houses near the water, including the one I now faced, and on the other to inland estates set back among trees and spacious lawns. The mansions were very far apart: if you were in one, you would have the impression that you were alone in a vast, water-edged countryside with no neighbors for miles. These people paid for Long Island's most desirable real estate, but, more than that, they paid for complete privacy. And that is exactly what they had.

The car I'd half-expected to see on the road near the gates of the Masterson/Vale place was nowhere in sight. Good; I was alone here, and I would be relatively unobserved. But only relatively, I knew. Walter Vale was in Japan, and his wife was obviously not at home. Jimmy, in the other car I'd rented for the week, was not here watching the house, which meant that he was discreetly following Mrs. Vale somewhere, monitoring her movements. That left the servants in the house.

Sixteen years ago, at the time of Laura Vale's murder, there had only been a daily housekeeper and one live-in maid. Now, Walter was the long-standing president of a major corporation and his second wife, I'd recently learned, was a famous hostess and a major driving force behind several social groups, arts societies, and charities. There were four servants now, a daily housekeeper and three live-ins, two maids and a man who had several jobs, including chauffeur and groundskeeper. Ann Vale drove her own car, I knew, but she usually preferred to be driven. There was every chance that the man would be out with her now, which left three women in the main house.

I would have to be careful.

First, I inspected the wrought-iron gates. Chap had instructed me on what to look for, explaining that there are three basic types of home security; four, if you count human sentries. I looked for camera equipment of any kind, either video or infrared, mounted on the walls or in nearby trees: none. Then I checked the sides of the gates and as much as I could see of the walls for any wires that could trigger alarms. There was nothing of the sort, as far as I could tell. I smiled as I glanced at the gate itself, remembering my embarrassment when I'd asked Chap for the third type of security. He'd stared at me a moment, as people stare at backward children. Then he'd smiled.

''A chain and a padlock,'' he'd said.

My chances for a career as a notorious jewel thief are virtually nonexistent—as was any form of padlock on the wrought-iron before me. There was a metal latch in the center at waist height, and a keyhole that would presumably afford a basic deadbolt situation between the two halves of the gate. But I could see at a glance that it was currently unlocked. All I would have to do to get in was lift the latch and swing the gates inward.

I did not. I intended to gain access to the grounds, but not in so mundane a manner. I was here for a dry run, a dress rehearsal of sorts, and that is what I would achieve. Joe Wilder, laughing in the face of adversity.

Tick-tock, tick-tock . . .

I followed the wall to the left until it ended, some fifty yards from the gates. The side wall extended before me now, another fifty yards or so, to the sea wall along the edge of the promontory above the beach. There was a dirt track outside the wall, dividing the Masterson/Vale property from its nearest neighbor. I made my way down this track to a point about halfway between the drive and the sea wall.

I loved climbing trees when I was a child in St. Thomas. This was probably a good thing, as I was about to do it again. Not that I wanted to, but it seemed to be my best chance. There was a tall, gnarled gray tree halfway along the side wall with thick, strong limbs. One of these extended over the high stone wall, mere inches from the top.

It was also, ironically, almost directly above a little green wooden door in the wall. This door was nearly invisible through the vines that covered this stretch of the stone, and it was firmly locked. So, it would have to be the tree.

I removed my gloves and winter coat and dropped them at the base of the tree, and I immediately started to shiver in the cold. Deciding that quick action was the only cure, I jumped up, grabbed the overhanging limb, and began the slow, ungraceful struggle to get my legs up to where my arms were. This took two false starts and the better part of five minutes, including a brief stop to catch my cigarette smoke–tinged breath. At last I was on top of the branch, hugging it tightly as it began to sag under my weight. The alarming bending increased as I shimmied out toward the top of the wall, and just before I dropped to the stone I heard a slight cracking sound. I lay atop the wall, clutching both sides of it, waiting for the panic to subside. A swift glance down at the ground inside the wall prompted another quick decision: don't look down. Just jump. I sat up on the wall, swung my legs over the side, and plummeted nearly ten feet to the manicured grass. The automatic tuck-and-roll maneuver that had once garnered praise for the thirteen-year-old Joe Wilder in gymnastics class in St. Thomas had lost most of its grace but none of its effectiveness in twenty-four years: I sat up on the lawn, winded but still breathing, my body outraged but whole.

I was inside the compound.

First, I turned around to inspect the door in the wall behind me. A sliding deadbolt just under the old-fashioned, rusted brass knob was all that was keeping it locked. Good: I could leave more comfortably than I had entered.

Then I turned back to face the estate. Ignoring the brief thought that I would ache like hell the next morning, I began to crawl forward on my hands and knees, scurrying toward the nearest clump of trees. I stood up behind one of them and peered around it. The big yellow house with the red clay-tiled roof and black wrought-iron second story

balconies stood in the distance across the statue-dotted
lawn, basking in the bright noonday sunlight. In the fore-
ground, not twenty feet from me, was the swimming pool.
Beside the sundeck stood the object of my intrusion, the
famous guest cottage. It was painted the same mustard yellow as the big house, and it had a matching red-tiled roof.

Scanning the windows of the main house that were visible to me from this vantage place, I took a deep breath and
began to run. I sprinted across the grass between the
trees to the side of the little outbuilding. I waited a few
seconds, listening. No cries from sharp-eyed parlormaids,
no running footsteps, no sudden wail of police sirens. Nothing. My pulse steadied itself, my breathing slowed to nor-
mal, and I crept around to the back of the cottage. There
was a door here, and two small windows, but all were
firmly locked. I would have to try my luck in front, in full
view of the house.

I hope that spies and secret agents are well paid for their
work, because there is no dignity in it, and the cost on the
nerves is tremendous. Hugging the rough yellow stucco
walls, I slid around the side of the poolhouse to the front
and dropped once more to my knees. There was a large,
top-opening wooden bin at this side corner, with a heavy
padlock at the top edge. I knelt behind this, peering around
it at the main house, inhaling the pungent scent of chlorine.
This was obviously the storage locker for the chemicals and
filters and long-handled sieves, all the necessities of a well-
tended swimming pool.

There was nothing I could see at any of the distant windows of the mansion, so I took a deep breath and crawled.
Creep, creep, wriggle, wriggle, more painful now because
I was on a sidewalk instead of soft grass. I arrived at the
front door—or, rather, at the bottom of it—and reached up
to the knob. It turned in my hand and the door swung silently inward. With another swift glance over my shoulder
toward the main house, I crawled inside and stood up.

The first thing I became aware of was the odd silence,

not merely the quiet of an empty room but of one that had been empty for a long time. It is a silence unlike any other. Of course, I now know that the room had not been empty recently, far from it, which leads me to the question of ghosts. I've never been certain how much I believe in the supernatural, but I know from experience the strange power that can emanate from a place where violence has occurred. Perhaps the poolhouse was haunted.

Aside from the atmosphere, it was a perfectly ordinary place. I was in a rather large room with white walls and a bare cement floor. The furniture was simple, tasteful, and expensive; one armchair, a simple cherrywood coffee table, and a beautiful mahogany rocking chair in the corner. A small wooden dining table and two chairs stood near the kitchenette along the back wall. Bookshelves lined a side wall, and a tiny reading desk with a telephone and a shaded brass lamp on it stood nearby. The other side wall was taken up by a fireplace, with an antique screen and grate. A wrought-iron, wagon-wheel chandelier with six lamp fixtures hung from the center of the ceiling, and there was a standing brass lamp next to the rocking chair. Two small doors near the bookshelves led to a closet and a bathroom. There was a picture window in the front wall next to the door. If the royal blue and white striped curtains were opened, there would be a lovely view of the pool and the mansion beyond it. But the curtains were drawn, and it was dark in the little house.

I went over to the lamp on the reading desk and switched it on, and the weird, otherworldly feeling immediately dispersed. The bodies and the bloodstains were long gone. It was just a room, and a lovely one at that.

And it would do quite nicely.

I gazed around the still, pretty place for a few moments, committing it to memory. I lifted the receiver of the little princess phone and held it to my ear: dial tone. Good. Then I switched off the lamp and went back over to the door. I

opened it slowly and peered cautiously out at the main
house before dropping to my knees, crawling out, and closing the door behind me. Now it was just a matter of re-
turning the way I had come. I actually sighed in relief as I
began to creep and wriggle away on my hands and knees.
I had made it approximately two creeps and one wriggle
along the side of the house when I suddenly came face-to-
face with a very large dog.

If you have ever suddenly been face-to-face with a very
large dog, you may appreciate my surprise. He was a red-
dish-yellow color, and he had big, expressive brown eyes.
The eyes were staring into mine, wary, curious. We both
remained quite still, staring, for what was probably ten seconds but felt like ten minutes.

I have always appreciated my mother, but never more
than at that moment. I grew up in a house with many animals, half of them dogs. I knew what to do.

"Hello," I said in a soft, straightforward tone of voice.
"My name is Joe. Who are you?"

He cocked his head a little, watching me as I rose slowly
to my feet.

"I guess you must belong to the Vales," I said, never
looking away, keeping my tone conversational. Show them
no aggression and no fear, and nine out of ten animals will
remain calm. Please, God, I thought, let him be one of the
nine. "I think you must be a setter. What a beautiful coat
you have. I wish I knew your name. But I don't know your
name, and I really have to go now. I hope we meet again
soon. Wouldn't that be nice? . . ."

I would have to go around him. I took a careful step
backward, never breaking eye contact, and moved slowly
in a half-circle toward the woods. I continued to speak, but
I don't remember what I said. He turned with me, slowly,
watching, the curious expression never wavering. When my
back was toward the distant wall, I began to walk backward. One step, then another, slowly, slowly, always keeping my empty hands in plain sight, always looking directly

into his eyes. He watched, making no attempt to follow. I'd made it about twenty steps backward when it happened. I ran smack into the trunk of a tree. Reflexively, my arms flew up to steady my balance.

That's when my luck ran out. With a low growl and a flash of big white teeth, the setter sprang forward.

I ran. I made it back through the trees in considerably less time than I had come. The dog ran after me, barking loudly. As the wall arrived before me, I actually considered a running leap to the top before I remembered about the gate. I aimed straight for the ivied green door, reaching out for it. I yanked the deadbolt to the side, grabbed the knob, twisted and pulled. With a small screech of protest, the door opened. I hurled myself through it and reached back to slam it shut, just in time. The wooden beams actually shivered with the impact as ninety pounds of angry animal smashed against the other side.

There was a sharp yelp of surprise or pain, followed by an ominous silence. Oh, God, I thought, he's hurt. I was reaching for the knob to open the door and see if he was all right when the barking began again. It was much louder this time. He was obviously standing there, facing the door in that charming way big dogs have, barking his head off.

Thank you very much, Chap Lannigan. I had just discovered Home Security System Number Five.

And a most effective system, I must say. My first instinct was to run, but then I thought better of it. Not that it mattered: I crept as quietly as possible along the outside of the high wall in the direction of the road, and the barking on the other side moved with me. Superdog, the Hound of Hell, complete with X-ray hearing. We traveled slowly down the wall that way for several yards, I creeping and he barking. I had just convinced myself that the best course of action was to cut and run when the other sound arrested me.

"Max! *Max*! Come here, you naughty dog!"

It was a woman—a young one, judging from her voice—

with a pronounced West Indian accent. Not St. Thomas, though; somewhere farther down the island chain. Trinidad? Wherever she was from, she was now standing somewhere between the dog and the house, probably near the swimming pool. I flattened myself against the wall and held my breath. The barking immediately stopped.

"Come *here*, Max! How many times have I told you not to bother the squirrels?!"

Squirrels, indeed, Madam! I thought as Max gave a sharp yip of greeting and thumped heavily away from the other side of the wall in the direction of the housekeeper or maid or whatever she was. I was actually chuckling softly to myself, more with relief than with humor, as I stepped away from the wall.

A hand with sharp nails immediately clapped down on my left shoulder.

I must have jumped about a foot, nearly crying out as I whirled around to face my captor. There was nobody there. I felt a sharp scratch on my shoulder and saw a flash of something gray and bushy next to my face, and then the disembodied hand leaped down from me and streaked away behind me, across the dirt road into the neighboring estate. I turned around just in time to see it disappear.

Squirrel. So, I had not been the only object of Max's angry barking. He'd chased me through the wall and the squirrel to the top of it. Then the squirrel, in quite understandable terror, had used me as a springboard between the top of the wall and the ground.

I still don't know why this should have struck me as funny. All I know is that I began to laugh. I ran back to the tree and collected my coat and gloves, not even bothering to put them on as I staggered away down the road, laughing insanely and gasping for breath, all the way to the car.

THIRTEEN

One Life to Live

He was a perfectly nice man in a perfectly nice house.

It was a pretty house on a pretty street in a pretty, upper-middle-class neighborhood in Syosset, a fashionable distance from the turnpike. I remembered this attractive town from my college days, and I was pleased to see that the ensuing years had been relatively kind to it, had not affected it as badly as they had affected so many other bedroom communities. Syosset would never be *the* place to live—even in this particular part of Long Island—but it was still a very pleasant place.

I pulled over to the curb across from the driveway that led up to the residence, a two-story combination of fitted stones and white wood siding. I glanced at my watch: three-fifteen. I was fifteen minutes late, which was hardly surprising, all things considered. When I'd planned today's excursion, I'd figured just enough time for the Davis dealership and the house in Oyster Bay, and I'd even figured in traveling times and an hour for lunch before arriving here in Syosset. No such luck. Getting into the grounds of the estate by means of a tree and meeting a rowdy setter were two details I had not foreseen. My stomach gave a low growl as I got out of the car, crossed the street, and made my way up to the front door.

He was waiting for me. No sooner had I rung the door-bell than the door was opened. Later, when I went back over the strange, rather sad interview in my mind, I realized that he had been watching anxiously from the front picture window for my arrival. He was even more nervous than I about our impending meeting.

"Mr. Wilder?" he whispered.

"Yes, doctor. Please call me Joe."

"Okay. I'm Ben, and I'm not really a doctor anymore. I'm retired. I'd rather everybody just call me Ben."

I nodded, and we shook hands. He had a firm grip, I noticed as I looked down at his hand in mine. A nice hand, well-formed and strong: an asset for a dentist, I should imagine.

He was about sixty, I guessed, and my first impression of him was one of sadness. There was something rather— I don't know, *wistful* in his expression, in his eyes, in the rather grim set of his mouth. He was a reasonably good-looking man, somewhat shorter than I, perhaps five-ten, and he had well-cut, light brown hair liberally streaked with gray. When he turned from the door to lead me inside, I noticed a small bald spot at the top in back, which he had vaguely attempted to cover with longer strands from the sides. He was wearing baggy brown cords and what must have been a favorite sweater; once a deep navy, it had faded with time and care to a dull, medium blue. The brown bed-room slippers on his feet had seen better days, as well. I concluded, as he preceded me into the rather large, well-furnished living room, that he probably did not have a wife.

Wrong.

"My wife, Martha, is working this afternoon," he said. "She's showing a house in Manhasset. Century 21, you know. I hope I remember everything she does when we have guests. Would you like a drink? We have coffee and

tea and soft drinks. And booze, of course. I was about to
have a beer.''

''Beer's fine,'' I said.

He nodded, waved me toward a couch, and left the room.
I sat down and looked around me. The furniture was fairly
new, I thought, and the walls of the room had recently been
painted. Everything was in shades of blue, from the pale
eggshell of the walls to the deep aquamarine wall-to-wall
carpet. The couch and chairs were upholstered in a striped,
light and dark blue pattern. The blue-curtained picture window afforded a view of the well-tended lawn. It was warm
here, and the air smelled faintly of wood soap and cinnamon.

Yes, there definitely was a wife. Martha, the realtor,
would have supervised the room's recent overhaul. I
guessed there would be a den nearby, and a kitchen and a
dining room, and two or three bedrooms upstairs. They had
probably been redone at the same time as this room, with
everything carefully chosen and coordinated by her. They
may have visited relatives or gone somewhere alone for a
week or two while the renovations took place. The Grand
Canyon, perhaps, or Disney World.

I realized, to my own surprise, that I was glad he had a
wife. Why am I glad about that? I wondered. I don't even
know him . . .

He came back into the room with two tall glasses of beer.
He handed me one and sat in a chair on the other side of
the coffee table.

''Do you mind if I smoke?'' he asked, picking up a pack
of cigarettes from the table.

''Not if I can join you,'' I replied. I fished in the pocket
of my coat, which I'd placed on the couch beside me. We
both lit up and sat regarding each other for a few moments.
I wondered where to begin.

''Do you have any children?'' I asked.

He hadn't been expecting that. His eyebrows went up as
he stared at me. Then he blinked and reached for his beer

glass. "I have a stepson, Martha's boy from her first marriage—or were you asking about *my* first marriage? That *is* what you came here to discuss, if I understood you on the phone yesterday. No, I—we didn't have children."

I nodded. We both drank from our glasses, then reached simultaneously for our cigarettes in the big round ashtray between us. The silence became strained. Now that I was here, I didn't know what to say to him.

He seemed to understand that, so he started us off. "I suppose you want to know everything I remember about her. Well, it's funny: I haven't really thought much about her in years. I could ask *you* why you called me, why you're interested. But I won't. The truth is, I don't much care. When I come to the end of my life, I guess I'll look back at it all. They say that's what people do, at the end. Well, when I look back, I'll see Martha. *She's* my wife, the only wife I—acknowledge."

I nodded again, watching him as he took another sip of beer. I took in the sight of this man, and the room around him, and the scent of cinnamon, wondering: why? Why did she leave you? Why didn't she love you? Why did she have to insist on having more? If, indeed, it *was* more. When he put the glass down, I leaned forward.

"I want to ask you a few questions," I said. "Your answers may be very important."

He sat back and grasped the arms of his blue-upholstered chair. Then, to my surprise, he grinned. It was a wide, generous smile that lit up his face and made sixteen years vanish in an instant. I wondered, vaguely, if he was responsible for his own perfect white teeth.

"Shoot," he said.

So we began. We spoke for nearly an hour. I asked several questions, and he answered them, frankly and, I thought, honestly. I was very careful, as I had been with Sarah Masterson in my mother's living room. I extracted the information I needed without giving away my game. Now, looking back, I can safely say that nothing I said that afternoon caused him a moment's anxiety or suspicion. This man, Ben, didn't deserve that: he deserved only peace and quiet, and to enjoy his well-earned retirement in his recently redecorated living room with his true and loyal wife. He had played a very minor part in the whole thing, after all, and now he was well out of it.

We sat there, drinking beer and smoking cigarettes while he told me everything he remembered. He spoke of love, and betrayal, and loss. There was anger afterward, he admitted, but soon it had faded. Well, that wasn't the word he used: he said it had *eroded*, bit by bit, until he simply didn't think about it anymore. At last he had met the estimable Martha, and she had helped him to get on with his life.

As he spoke of her, she became almost real to me, this great offstage character, this Martha. I never met her, never even saw her, but I have a picture of her in my mind. She is a handsome, smiling woman, gentle and generous and considerate, and her value is above rubies.

He talked, and I extracted information as delicately as he had once extracted teeth. My task was a relatively easy one, as it turned out. He never once asked me a question, or in any way displayed the slightest curiosity. As he'd told me at the beginning, he didn't much care. This was a good thing, I suppose. By the time I was finished, I knew everything. He would find out about it all soon enough, I reasoned, but I wouldn't be here to see it. I wouldn't have to see the pain in his eyes, or feel his self-recrimination, if there was any. I hoped there would be none.

At the end of our strange, rather sad interview, he glanced at his watch and rose, informing me that Martha would be home shortly. Then he asked me, very politely, to leave. He didn't want her to meet me here, he said, or to know that we had been discussing things of which she would disapprove.

I nodded and reached for my coat. At the door, I shook his hand and thanked him, and he rewarded me with another dazzling grin. I went out into the cold, down the driveway beside the lovely lawn and across the street to my car. As I drove away, I looked back once more.

He was standing in his doorway, waving, a perfectly nice man in a perfectly nice house.

FOURTEEN

My Ship Comes In

After leaving Long Island that afternoon, I joined the others at the hideout, Amber's apartment on East Tenth Street. My adventures throughout the day—the car dealership, the dog, the house in Syosset—had been full of surprises, and they seemed to have inured me to any further shocks. This probably explains why I merely shrugged and said hello when I found Sarah Masterson sitting with her granddaughter in Amber's living room.

"I'm afraid I couldn't stay away, after all," she said, her only attempt at explaining why she had defied my instructions. "But you needn't worry about my being followed here. I wasn't—*he* saw to that." She pointed at Chap Lannigan, who was slouched in an armchair nearby. "He brought me here."

I nodded. "Okay." I looked at my watch, aware of the gnawing pains in my empty stomach. It was five-thirty. "I realize it's unfashionably early, but I'd love some dinner."

Without a word, Jenny Hughes rose from her seat in a corner and went over to the telephone.

"I won't be able to join you," Sarah Masterson said. "I'm meeting people for dinner and the theater, and it's too late to cancel. In fact, I must leave right now." She turned to Emma and Stan on the couch. "You two be careful. This will all be over soon." Looking directly at me, she added, "Saturday."

With that, she kissed her granddaughter and rose. Chap, with a nod from me, escorted her out. As he opened the apartment door and held it for her, she smiled at him.

"You know, Mr. Lannigan," she said, "I'm quite in love with you."

And she was gone. I watched her go, thinking, *Tick-tock, tick-tock . . .*

When Jenny was finished ordering in food on the phone, she caught my eye, made a little hand gesture beckoning me, and went into Amber's kitchen, away from the others. I followed.

"I had a rather odd phone call at my place this morning," she said, leaning back against the kitchen counter and folding her arms across her chest. "Well, not odd, exactly. *Mysterious* is a better word. You and I have an appointment uptown later this evening."

I frowned. "Is this relevant?"

She shook her head, glancing toward the living room. She kept her voice low. "I don't know. We'll see. But we're going. You were specifically asked for, and I promised."

I nodded. "Okay."

Then I went back into the living room and turned my attention to the two people on the couch. I looked at the pale, nervous woman beside her husband, who still sported gauze bandages over most of the right side of his face. I thought about her family and friends, and about her job at Masterson Electronics, and about his brokerage firm. I thought about their life together in the lovely apartment on Madison and Sixty-fifth she had once shared with Jenny. I thought about the baby, growing even now inside her, due on August 24, or thereabouts. And as they gazed silently up at me from the couch, I thought about all the rest of it, everything I knew.

The car on the FDR Drive. The aspirin in the sleeping pill bottle. The near-fatal crash on the exit ramp from the Brooklyn Bridge.

Her sister, Sarah Vale, waiting on West End Avenue for a worthless lover who would probably never arrive. Her mother, Laura Vale, running through the rain. Laura's worthless lover, Michael Trent, waiting in the darkened poolhouse. His mother, sixteen years later, weeping for him in her living room in Florida, her memories of him preserved in lemonade-tinged gin. A perfectly nice man, a dentist, in a perfectly nice house in Syosset, Long Island.

It's time, I thought. It's time for all of this to stop.

I sank slowly into the chair across from Emma and her husband and lit a cigarette. Jenny came out of the kitchen to join us, and a few minutes later Chap came in, having put Mrs. Masterson in a cab. We all sat around Amber's coffee table, waiting for dinner. While we waited, I told them everything. Everything I had done, everything I had learned, everything I was planning to do. I spoke for a long time.

When I was finished, there was a brief silence as they all considered it. Then Emma said, "You have no proof of any of this, do you?"

I smiled and gave a little shrug. "No, I don't—but I know I'm right."

She nodded slowly. "I think perhaps you are, but do you think your plan will work?"

Another smile, another shrug. I was getting good at that.

"We'll see, won't we?" I said.

Tick-tock, tick-tock . . .

Three hours later, at about ten o'clock, Jenny and I got out of a cab on Lexington Avenue in the mid-Fifties. The hotel on the corner there had once been exclusively for women, but changing times had warranted changing policies. It had never been a grand place, but it had always been respectable. As we entered the dark, carpeted, old-fashioned lobby, I had an immediate impression of shabby gentility. The rooms would be in the upper-middle price range to suit the predominantly upper-middle-class clientele, and they would be reasonably attractive and very clean. Yet, somehow, as with all big hotels that never quite made it to the top, there was something distinctly sad about it. Something forlorn and rather unappealing.

This impression was only made stronger as we entered the quiet, dark lounge on the corner, just off the lobby. It was a big room, with tall, wide windows framed by dark green velvet curtains affording a view of the constant Lexington Avenue traffic. The walls and the bar that ran the length of one side of the room were paneled in dark-colored wood, and the tables and green velvet-upholstered chairs matched them. A middle-aged man in a faded dinner jacket sat at the baby grand piano in one corner by the windows, softly playing Broadway show tunes that had been hits when this room had last been popular: Irving Berlin, Noël Coward, the Gershwins. The round glass fishbowl on top of the piano in front of him was empty. Four of the twenty tables were occupied by two silent couples, a silent group of four, and a lone woman. Two beefy Midwest businessman types sat at the long bar, trading undoubtedly dirty jokes that were undoubtedly as old as the music with the bored, red-jacketed bartender.

The lone woman was Rachel Cohen, Jenny and Emma's friend from college. She was sitting at a table in the darkest part of the room, farthest from the piano. She was wearing a black sequined cocktail dress, and her dark hair fell loose about her mostly bare shoulders. She smiled and waved to us as we came in. When we arrived at the table she jumped up from her seat, and she and Jenny did the huggy-kissy thing. Then she shook my hand and we all sat.

Rachel insisted that we all have the "house special," which I ordered from the bored, red-jacketed waiter. Then she leaned forward, her elbows on the edge of the table.

"Thanks for coming, Jen, and thanks for bringing him. I—I don't really know how to say this." She took a breath and plunged. "Okay. Emma called me last night. It's the first I've heard from her since the accident. I tried reaching her at home, and I even called both Sarahs, but no one would tell me where she was. But Sarah the Younger *did* tell me something rather—disturbing. She said she was getting married. To Craig. Well, that was kind of bothering me, and then, last night, Emma called out of the blue. She told me she was in hiding, she wouldn't say where, and then—then she told me what's been going on. About the accident on the Brooklyn Bridge not really being an accident, and about the FDR Drive a few weeks ago, and the aspirin thing. And I got to thinking—"

At this point the waiter arrived and deposited three tall glasses on the table before us. The liquid in them was bright green, and the glasses were garnished with orange slices and maraschino cherries on plastic swizzle sticks. The "house special." Rachel grabbed hers and downed nearly half of it. Jenny and I exchanged glances, politely sipped something horribly sweet, and never touched our glasses again. I actually pushed mine away from me as I leaned forward.

"Rachel, go back a bit. Why were you disturbed to hear that Sarah Vale is planning to marry Craig Davis?"

"Well, I—" She stopped, glancing over at Jenny. "Oh, God, Jen, I don't know if I'm doing the right thing. I may just be gossiping."

Jenny reached over and took her friend's hand. "Tell us."

Rachel nodded. "Okay. Emma told me that you guys were, you know, helping her out. Looking into this, is what she said. So, it's about Craig. Back when Emma was dating him, he had this occasional bartending job at one of those places in the theater district." She looked around the room. "Kind of like this, only with living people. I'm sorry about

this place—I only asked you to meet me here because I
live right down the block, and I didn't know how soon I
could get rid of our dinner guests. I don't want Dave hearing any of this, he'd think I'm just telling tales out of
school. Anyway, Craig worked at this theater bar, and
Emma used to drag us all down there to visit him while he
worked. Dave and I became friendly with the other bartender there, an old character actor named Morty who's
very funny. We still stop in there occasionally to see him.
Well, Morty never liked Craig, and he didn't like the fact
that Emma was seeing him. One night back then, he got a
little sloshed and told Dave and me something very interesting. He said that Craig was seeing someone else, and we
should discourage Emma from getting serious about him.
He didn't know who the other woman was, he said, but
she'd been in a couple of times when both of them were
working. She and Craig would have these make-out ses-
sions and long, whispered conversations at one end of the
bar. And one night they had an argument. Morty didn't hear
any of it, but the woman went storming out of the place,
and Craig was furious—''

"Rachel," I interjected, looking pointedly at my watch.
"I'm sorry, but I've had a very long day—"

She brought up her hands in surrender. "Okay, okay, I
talk too much. I always have. Long story short: Emma
broke up with Craig soon after that, and I never saw fit to
mention this, to her or anyone. When Craig took up with
Sarah, I'd pretty much forgotten about it. And I don't much
care for Sarah, anyway. Well, a couple of months ago we
stopped in to see Morty, and he had news. Sarah Vale had
just hired him to bartend at a party she gave at her place
on West End Avenue. Her family and friends—and Craig
was there, of course. Well, that's when Morty saw her
again. The woman from the bar. It had been a few years,
but he was certain it was the same one." Her eyes widened,
and her voice dropped to a whisper. "This is *so* weird . . ."

Jenny and I were both leaning forward now, staring.

At last she said it. Even though I knew what she was going to say, a little thrill coursed through me. Jenny closed her eyes, nodding to herself. I sat back in my chair, gazing off toward the other side of the room.

The pianist chose that very moment to segue from "September Song" into another Kurt Weill classic. "My Ship" from *Lady in the Dark*. In a soft, gravelly voice, he began to croon the lyrics. I watched him, listening, remembering that day a week before when this very song had played in the background, in Emma Vale Smith's apartment. And I remembered what Emma had said then, about Michael Trent:

"I knew he was the pool lifeguard at the club, but we kids rarely went to the pool. We were always on the beach. Mother and her girlfriends hung out at the pool . . ."

My ship had come in.

I nudged Jenny's knee under the table. When she looked over at me, I drew my eyebrows briefly together. Be cool, my look said, be noncommittal. She nodded and smiled brightly over at her friend.

"That's very interesting, " she said. "But I'm not certain it has any bearing on—on Emma's problem. I—I think we'll know more tomorrow. Won't we, Joe?"

"Oh, yes," I said quickly, smiling at Rachel Cohen. Her face relaxed. Good. "We'll know more tomorrow. But until then, let's just keep all this to ourselves, okay?"

Rachel smiled and nodded. She finished her "house special," whatever it was, and Jenny immediately steered us off into small talk, mostly old college stories to which I only half-listened, smiling distractedly as they giggled and gossiped. And all the while I was thinking:

Tomorrow.

When we finally rose to leave, the two women preceded me to the door that led to the depressing, old-fashioned lobby. As I crossed the room behind them, I had a sudden, overwhelming impulse. I left them at the doorway and made my way over to the piano. I pulled out my wallet and dropped two crisp twenty dollar bills in the empty fishbowl.

The pianist smiled up at me. "Thank you very much, sir! Do you have a request?"

I smiled right back. "No, I don't. You just played my favorite song."

FIFTEEN

Setting the Stage

The following day, Friday, was drab and overcast. Enormous black clouds crouched ominously above New York, and there was a feel in the cold air of imminent rain. Despite the weather, it was a busy day for Jenny, Chap, and me. Me, mostly. At ten o'clock that morning, I went to see a real estate woman, a Mrs. Wahlberg, in her office on Hudson Street a few blocks south of my apartment. I talked with her for an hour. Two hours later, at one o'clock, I met my two colleagues at Jenny's apartment in Gramercy Park.

It had never occurred to me before, what an unlikely trio we were. I sat in that pretty West Indian apartment, looking from the hulking blond giant sprawled on the bamboo couch to the lovely Caribbean woman seated so elegantly in the rattan fan chair. What, I suddenly wondered, did the three of us have in common? We barely knew each other, and our backgrounds were divergent, to say the least. Jenny and I had grown up in St. Thomas, but our paths had rarely crossed until after I moved away. And Chap—well, he was a cipher. I knew what he did for a living; I'd even seen him in action. He had a room in the Village, and he dated

a pretty aspiring actress, and he liked Mozart. That was all
I knew about him, really.

What struck me as odd about all this was the realization
that I felt perfectly at ease with them. I had already asked
Jenny Hughes to join me in my proposed venture, and I
would soon give Chap Lannigan the same offer. I had no
qualms about that. I trusted them. There, in that apartment
with two relative strangers, I was comfortable.

What's more, they seemed to be comfortable, too. I'm
not sure why I say that: I just felt that it was true. Even as
I looked from one to the other, studying them, they were
both leaning forward, watching me as though they were
waiting for me to make my next pronouncement.

So I made it.

"Okay," I said to them. "It happens tonight. Chap, I
want you to make a phone call. They may recognize my
voice, but not yours."

Chap said nothing, but Jenny immediately asked, "A
phone call to whom?"

I explained, and the two of them listened attentively.
Then I went over to Jenny's telephone and dialed the number I had committed to memory. I would need to dial it
again, later. I handed the receiver to Chap.

He was perfect. When the phone was answered, he asked
for the person to whom he was to speak. He introduced
himself as "a friend," just as I had told him. There was a
pause while he waited, and then he began to talk again. In
a few terse sentences, he delivered the message and confirmed that it was understood, that the instructions would
be followed. Then he replaced the receiver and nodded.

"All set," he said.

I smiled. "Good. Now, here's what I want you to do
tonight . . ."

While I spoke, he listened in that way he has, staring off
into space while obviously not missing a single word.
When I was through, he didn't say anything. He merely
grunted once, which I took as an affirmative.

So, we were all clear on what would happen later, and it would—probably—go off without a hitch. I was satisfied with that, but Jenny apparently was not. She rose slowly from the rattan chair and wandered over to the nearest window. She stood there gazing out, her back to us. When she finally spoke, her voice was heavy with concern.

"Joe, I want you to be very careful tonight."

I caught Chap's eye. He shrugged. *Women*, the shrug said, as eloquently as if he had spoken it aloud. I stood up and went to stand beside Jenny at the window.

"I'll be careful," I told her.

She didn't look at me. She continued to stare out at the black clouds above the park. I wondered what she was thinking, but I was tactful enough not to ask. Emma Vale Smith was her friend, and I could just imagine how awful she felt. The clouds seemed to grow larger even as we watched them, filling the sky, blotting out the sun. There was a flash of light against the windowpanes, followed moments later by the low, distant rumble of thunder.

At last she said, "It's going to be a terrible night."

"Yes," I said. "I know."

It was a dark and stormy night.

That silly phrase keeps going through my mind, even now. It was the first thing I thought of when I read the accounts of the events sixteen years ago, and still it echoes down, informing everything.

The rain had already been falling for several hours when I drove out to the north shore of Long Island late that Friday night, and the Expressway was a mere blur through the headlights and the windshield wipers. The wind buffeted the car as I drove, augmented every few minutes by lightning and thunder. Another link, as if I needed one. Sixteen years ago and the present . . .

I thought briefly of Jenny Hughes, who would even now be with her friend in Amber's apartment. I tried to imagine the two women sitting side by side on the couch, waiting for news. It wasn't a very pleasant image, so I quickly dismissed it and concentrated on my own job.

My own job. I thought about that as I drove, the strange, even bizarre thing that I was racing out there to do. A week before, I had blithely informed Jenny of what I intended to do with the money that had been left to me. I'd even invented a name for it: the Mongoose Fund. It had seemed somehow romantic, dangerous, exciting. Now I realized the fascination it held for me, the glamor it promised. It represented everything I didn't have in my life. My only passions of late had been writing plays and novels. Aside from my family and a few friends and the occasional pleasant-but-not-very-important relationship with someone like Donna Crain, there was nothing in my life that truly *mattered*.

A writer's life is solitary. I'd always heard that, and now I know firsthand that it is true. But I intend to have more, to have my cake and eat it, as it were. I realized that just then, as I made my way through the terrible weather to Oyster Bay. I knew that I could do this strange, even bizarre thing before me. And when I was through, the lives of several people would improve. What I was doing would make a profound difference, to them and to me. It *mattered*.

Of course, I didn't know then how very close I was to death. If I had, I wonder what I would have done. Turn the car around? I hope not. I guess I'm afraid of a lot of things, but my biggest fear is cowardice. That's probably funny, and I might have laughed at the thought if I'd had it then. But I didn't: I was too busy ignoring my fear and pressing onward.

And then my journey was over. Through the slashing rain, I could just make out the dark shape of a car parked at the side of the road across from the gates of the estate. As I approached, its engine started and the headlights flashed on. The car came slowly by me on the road, and as it passed the big African-American man I knew only as Jimmy looked over at me. Our eyes met through the rain-streaked glass. He nodded once and drove away in the direction of New York City. The nod told me what I needed to know: everything was in place.

I drove to the end of the estate wall and turned down the little lane beside it that lead to the Sound. I switched off my headlights and moved slowly, cautiously down the dirt track until I saw the other car parked among the trees just inside the neighboring property. I pulled in beside the other car and parked. Just before I turned off the engine, I glanced at the dashboard clock: eleven twenty-three. The rain pattered down on the roof as I sat there breathing slowly in and out, preparing myself.

It's time, I thought. Now.

I buttoned the black raincoat over my black sweater and jeans, and pulled the hood up over my head. Then I was out of the car and across the lane, running toward the little green door in the side wall. The setter, Max, would be in for the night, and the rain would further mask my presence. I pushed the door open and went inside.

There were floodlights placed around the open expanse in front of the main house, bathing the lawn and the facade of the big yellow building in a wash of white light. I made my way swiftly through the darkness among the trees in the direction of the poolhouse. As I arrived at the door, I turned around to look at the mansion. The servants would be in the basement apartment by now, and the only lights inside the house shone from a pair of upstairs windows. I went into the poolhouse and closed the door behind me.

It wasn't entirely dark here. The outside lights shone on the curtains at the picture window, causing a dim glow on everything in the room. The couch, the armchair, the fireplace, the little kitchenette: I could just make it all out. I removed the dripping raincoat, dropped it on the couch, and moved to the reading desk near the bookshelves on the side wall. I switched on the little shaded lamp and reached for the telephone. I stood there, the receiver in my hand, remembering Chap's brief message on the phone that afternoon.

"I know what happened to Laura and Mike, and I know what happened to Craig Davis. Stay by your phone tonight. Do you understand me?"

With another long, deep breath, I punched in the numbers I'd committed to memory.

It was answered on the first ring. I spoke briefly and hung up, not even waiting for a reply. Then I went over to sit on the couch facing the front door. I got my cigarettes from the pocket of the raincoat, lit one, and sat there, waiting.

As I waited, I listened to the steady sound of the rain on the poolhouse roof. Every now and then there would be a flash of light against the drawn curtains, followed by a long, low rumble. This is how it was then, I mused. These were the sounds outside, sixteen years ago . . .

"How many of these people were around sixteen years ago?"

And with the sounds of the weather came the other sounds, the voices that had brought me here:

"You're Joseph Wilder, and I'm a fan of yours."

"Please call me Joe . . ."

"Chap."

"I beg your pardon?"

"My name. It's Chap, not Charles. I hate Charles . . ."

"Mrs. Trent."

"Call me Dolly. Everybody does . . ."

"Tell me about Sarah."

"Grammy?"

"No, I mean your sister, Sarah Vale."

"Oh. Her. Two women: one name. And they couldn't be more different if they tried . . ."

It was all about names, the significance of names. I remembered brunch at Emma's apartment two weeks ago:

"All these people were here?"

"Yes. Thirty-two people, to be exact. Cocktails, a catered buffet, the inevitable champagne toast—Stan's father did

that, because Dad and Ann were gone by then."

"Ann?"

"My stepmother . . ."

I remembered Emma's speech, several days later:

"I knew he was the pool lifeguard at the club, but we kids rarely went to the pool. We were always on the beach. Mother and her girlfriends hung out at the pool . . ."

I remembered the final entry in Laura Vale's diary:

Meeting M at poolhouse at 12. Telling him NO MORE . . . *If W ever found out, it would kill him . . . It's the right thing to do, the only thing to do. A just said so, and I agreed.*

I remembered Rod Hutchinson, staring out over Tampa Bay:

"He was my best friend, you know? We grew up together. I thought I really knew him, but I obviously didn't. He beat the shit out of me and ran off with Marie—that was her name, Marie. A year later he killed that woman, Laura Vale, and then he offed himself. God, I still don't *believe it!"*

And my reply:

"No, I don't believe it, either."

There was another flash of lightning and another roll of thunder, and all the voices came together in my head, a symphony of sound:

"How many of these people . . ."

"Ann?"

"My stepmother . . ."

"How many of these people were around . . ."

"Mother and her girlfriends . . ."

"That was her name, Marie. . . ."

"Oh. Her. Two women: one name. And they couldn't be more different . . ."

"How many of these people were around sixteen years ago?"

One last outrageous, deafening crack of thunder, then everything was silent. I looked around the room, thankful for the dim light from the little lamp on the desk. When I had first come in here yesterday, I'd felt a presence, as if the two people who'd died here sixteen years ago still remained, waiting for something. Now, I could feel their presence again, and I knew that what they were waiting for was justice. I didn't know if Michael Trent deserved justice, but Laura Vale . . .

Laura Vale, who had always loved to dance. Who loved Elvis Presley and Broadway musicals. Whose favorite novel was, ironically, the tragedy of an incurable romantic, a woman who would rather die than accept the fact that she was ordinary, that her life had been unremarkable. Laura Vale, who so closely identified herself with her heroine that she named her first child after her.

Sixteen years ago, on a night such as this one, Laura Vale had sat at the little desk in the living room, staring out at the storm. She had probably strained her ears to hear any sounds from upstairs as she scrawled her last, feverish musings in her journal. Then, when she knew that she could put it off no longer, she had grabbed her beige raincoat and her black umbrella and run out into the storm, into that wild night, to meet her own romantic fate.

As I waited in the poolhouse, I saw her again: running, running breathlessly through the rain, a little smile of triumph or of righteousness lighting up her face, filling her with the vital, overwhelming energy that was her most notable trait. I wanted to be there, to have been there, to plant myself directly in her path and bar her way. To hold out my hands before her and tell her to stop, *stop*, your friend is not your friend, your love is not your love. But I am not there, cannot be there, so she continues on her way unchecked, hurrying out of the garage and flying down the sidewalk, around the swimming pool, arriving at last at this door before me.

Laura Vale, I thought again as the vision faded and I came back to the present, leaning forward to crush out my cigarette in the big, round, heavy brass ashtray on the coffee table. Laura Vale . . .

Then the door swung slowly open, and Laura Vale came into the room.

I couldn't see her distinctly. The floodlights from the grounds outside backlit her, forming a halo of light around her silhouette in the doorway. She dropped her umbrella—useless in the wind outside—and removed her beige raincoat. The light glinted in her wet blond hair and on her white dress, the dress she'd been wearing when they found her the next day.

"Hello," the apparition said, smiling.

I rose slowly to my feet as she stepped forward into the light from the lamp, and now I saw her clearly.

Emma Vale Smith.

SIXTEEN

Woman in the Dark

"For Heaven's sake, Joe, you look as if you've seen a ghost!"

I stared.

"I know I'm not supposed to be here," she said, still smiling as she came over to me, "but I just had to see this for myself."

I stared.

"God, I hate this place!" she whispered, glancing around as she dropped her wet raincoat on top of mine. "I haven't even been in here since—what? What is it, Joe?"

I blinked. Then I found my voice.

"What the hell are you doing here?" I croaked. "You're supposed to be—how did you get here?"

Her smile became mischievous. "In a cab. I came in through the side wall, just like you said you were going to do. Don't worry, nobody saw me. I let the cab go, though. I hope you can take me back to—"

"Where's Jenny?" I cried.

Now Emma blinked. "At Amber's with Stan, I suppose. He was asleep when I left. I'm afraid I told a little fib. I said I had a headache, and I sent Jenny out for a bottle of

Tylenol. Amber's into holism, you know, she doesn't have any medicine in her—''

"You've got to get out of here," I said. "*Now*!"

She blinked again, and her smile faded, replaced by an expression I'd never seen on her face before. I can only describe it as grim determination.

"You don't get it, do you?" she said. "The white dress, the beige raincoat. I found them in Amber's closet, and they're rather perfect, aren't they? You're a playwright: set the stage. You thought you could just march in here and say—what?" She shook her head. "No, Joe, I'm not going anywhere. *I'm* Laura Vale, and *you're* Michael Trent, and *we* are about to scare the life out of—listen!"

She cocked her head, glancing over at the open door. Through the sound of the pouring rain I could hear it now, as well, the unmistakable clicking of rapidly approaching footsteps.

"No—" I began, but it was as far as I got. Emma turned back to me.

"We're on!" she whispered. Then, in one swift, graceful move, she stepped forward, threw her arms around my neck, and kissed me on the lips.

A flash of lightning, a crack of thunder. I stood there, paralyzed, feeling the intense pressure of her lips on mine as the voices flooded in again.

"How many of these people were around . . ."

"Ann?"

"My stepmother . . ."

"That was her name, Marie . . ."

"Oh. Her. Two women: one name. And they couldn't be more different . . ."

Through the haze, through my panic, I was aware that the footsteps had stopped. Emma's lips were crushing mine. I couldn't breathe. Beyond the blond hair pressed against my face I saw the shape, the backlit figure silhouetted in the doorway. In the dim light in the room, we obviously created the desired effect. The dark figure uttered a loud gasp.

No, I thought as Emma stepped back from me and turned toward the door. I have to stop this. I have to do something . . .

"Two women: one name . . ."

Emma stared at the figure in the doorway, raising her hands dramatically to her face. "You!"

Then the silhouetted figure, the woman in the dark, stepped forward into the light.

Two women, I thought. One name.

Or one woman with two names.

A just said so, and I agreed . . .

A for Annemarie.

Ann.

Marie.

Annemarie Nevins.

"How many of these people were around . . ."

The other day at Amber's apartment, between dinner and Trivial Pursuit, I'd asked Emma two questions:

"Did your father marry Annemarie Nevins?"

"Yes."

"And were they having an affair before your mother died?"

"I don't know."

But someone else had known. He'd told me all about it, in his house in Syosset. Dr. Benjamin Nevins.

"How many of these people were around sixteen years ago?"

Ann Vale—Annemarie Nevins—stood just inside the doorway, as she had done on that night sixteen years ago. And now, as then, she brought her right hand up.

I moved. I grabbed Emma's arm and shoved her down onto the couch. Then I threw myself down on top of her.

The two explosions came so quickly, so close together, that they almost sounded like one. The first bullet slammed into the wall of the kitchenette directly behind where Emma had been standing a split second before. The second went into the top of the couch inches above my head. I lay on top of Emma, clutching her to me, bracing myself for the third shot.

It never came. I heard another gasp and a little scream of pain, followed by the thump of the gun hitting the cement floor. Then silence. Still I stayed there, shielding Emma's body with my own, until I heard the soft, familiar voice: unruffled, unconcerned, almost bored.

"Okay, you can get up now."

I let go of Emma and got up from the couch. Ann Vale stood before me, wincing in pain, her right arm pinned behind her back. Beside her stood the huge, reassuring, soaking wet form of Chap Lannigan.

"Hi," he said.

I nodded. "Hello." I leaned down and picked up the gun, then turned around to help a terrified Emma Vale Smith to her feet. She was very pale, and my first thought was for the baby. "Are you all right?"

She reached up to place a trembling hand on her stomach. "Yeah, I'm okay."

"Good. Now go over to that phone and call Jenny. She must be frantic."

Without another word, she did as she was told.

I turned back to the others, pointing at the armchair across from the couch. "There."

Chap led Mrs. Vale over and thrust her down into the chair. I handed him the gun. Then he went over to the door, closed it, and leaned back against it, the gun in his hand dangling at his side. I sank down onto the couch, reaching in my coat for another cigarette.

She was wearing a long blue raincoat over a dark maroon pantsuit, and her short black hair was plastered against her head. Though she was dripping wet, her expensive makeup had withstood the elements. Score one for Revlon. But even that worthy corporation could have done nothing to soften the expression on her angular face, in her big, dark eyes.

She looked murderous, and haughty, and desolate, all at the same time. She looked horrible. She watched in silence as I lit the cigarette and settled back on the couch.

"So," I said in an offhand, conversational tone of voice, "where's Craig Davis?"

Ann—or Marie, or Annemarie, or whatever she wanted to call herself—continued to stare at me in complete silence, her perfect red lips pressed tightly together.

I raised my eyebrows, just to let her know how amused but otherwise unaffected I was by her silence. "Okay, let me guess. He probably went the way of Michael Trent, am I right? You brought Trent up here from Tampa and got him the job at the yacht club. You fairly well stage-managed his eventual affair with Laura Vale. Your unhappy, dissatisfied friend, your *rich* friend. I'll bet you used to meet Michael Trent right here, in this room—when he wasn't using it with Laura, that is."

I looked behind me. Emma was on the phone, reassuring Jenny. She couldn't hear this part. Good.

"Meanwhile," I went on, "you took up with Walter. Oh, it was perfect. I really have to hand it to you. You and your lover, Michael Trent, are going to get rid of his other lover, Laura Vale. Then you're going to marry *your* other lover, Walter Vale. And, after a reasonable amount of time, Walter has an accident, and, lo and behold, you and Michael will have—what is it? Nearly half a billion." I leaned forward, watching her. "At least, that's what *Michael* thinks. But you know otherwise. All the while you and he are planning to have Laura murdered by a mysterious, anonymous lover, *you're* setting *him* up as the very *un*-anonymous lover. Which is exactly what he was! Did you *buy* Laura that diary? Encourage her to confess everything in it? Oh, you are some piece of work, Annemarie! May I call you that? It makes it all *so* much easier."

I heard a low chuckle from the doorway. She stared some more; I smiled some more. I took a long drag on the cigarette and continued.

"So you got them both to come here that night, at midnight. September 14. You were on the phone with her when Walter went up to bed. And the minute he disappeared, you told her. 'Break it off with Michael, Laura. It's the only thing to do. *I'll* call him and tell him to meet you in the poolhouse at midnight.' Which is exactly what you did. You told him to kill her—with a gun you probably supplied. Was she already dead when you arrived here that night, Annemarie? Probably. And you took the gun from his hand. 'It's done, darling! Now we'll have everything,' you assure the poor, coked-up slob as you step forward to embrace him. And, *bang*!" I slammed my hand down on the coffee table. She winced. "Exit Michael Trent. Then you place the gun in his hand and run off home to Syosset, to finalize your own divorce proceedings. You are appropriately shocked, and after an appropriate period of mourning, you become the second Mrs. Vale. Which is when you learn about Bradley Masterson's will."

She slowly raised one eyebrow, but her contemptuous gaze was no longer directed at me. She was looking past me, over my shoulder. I turned my head. Emma had hung up the phone, and she now stood behind the couch, leaning over, her elbows resting on the back.

"May I take over for a while?" Emma asked.

I grinned up at her. "I wish you would. I'm getting tired of hearing my own voice."

She fixed her stepmother with a cold stare, and her voice matched her expression. "I've always wondered why you hated me. Why you hated *us*, my sister and me. Now I know: Brad Masterson's will. You murdered two people— and you were planning to murder my father—for money that would never have been yours in any event. It bypassed Walter and came directly to me. And if anything were to happen to me, it would go to Sarah. Blood descendants." She shook her head, and her blond hair glistened in the soft light. "But you didn't know that when you married Father. So, you settled back with his not-inconsiderable fortune and waited. You waited for an opportunity to make history repeat itself. Another madcap heiress, and another handsome, amoral, desperate young man. Craig Davis.''

Annemarie Nevins Vale stood up. She jumped up from the chair and turned to the door. She'd actually taken a step toward it when she saw the enormous man who stood there raise his arm and point her own gun directly at her heart.

''Sit,'' he said.

She sank back into the chair. She stared up at Emma, finally breaking her silence.

''You stupid bitch!'' she hissed. ''It was *so* easy.''

''I'm sure it was,'' I said. ''I'm curious: how long did it take you to recruit Emma's lover?''

''Ha!'' she cried. It was a harsh, ugly sound. She raised her hand and pointed. ''I had him on that couch you're sitting on the second time I ever met him!''

I smiled at her. ''You realize, of course, that you're incriminating yourself . . .''

Her eyes widened, and then her mouth snapped shut again.

''Not that it matters,'' I continued blithely. ''You just attempted to murder the two of us. Chap saw the whole thing. Even if we can't pin Laura Vale or Michael Trent on you, you're going directly to jail, as they say in Monopoly.'' I leaned forward again. ''You might as well tell us where Craig is.''

She crossed her hands primly on her lap and pursed her lips.

''He's dead, isn't he?'' I said.

She stared at me some more. Emma came around the couch and stood before her. Only the coffee table separated them.

''Why, Ann?'' she cried. ''Why me? Why *now*?''

I rose to stand beside Emma. I reached over and took her trembling hand in mine. We both stared down at her stepmother in the chair.

''That's easy, Emma,'' I said. ''You broke up with Craig

before he could marry you, which threw a wrench in their plan. So she immediately positioned him with the next best thing, your sister. You have an accident, then Sarah has an accident—you see how it works? And the fortune is divided between the relatives by marriage: Mrs. Masterson, Walter Vale, and Craig. Then—Craig thinks—Walter has an accident, and Craig and Annemarie are stinking rich. Hell, two thirds of the Masterson fortune is about three hundred million. But then, Emma, a year ago, you screwed up the whole thing. You married Stan. And about two months ago, you had a party at your apartment. You announced to friends and family the one thing this woman didn't want to hear.''

Emma looked from Mrs. Vale to me. Then her hands came up to her mouth.

"Oh, my God!" she whispered. "The baby!"

"Bingo!" I said. "The baby. The new, undisputed heir. So Annemarie here excuses herself and ducks into the powder room. Next thing you know, you're in the hospital. Well, that doesn't work, so two weeks later Craig tries nudging you off the FDR Drive. Then, last Saturday, he tried it again. My word, Emma, you certainly are hard to kill!''

"Pardon me," she said, staring at the woman in the chair. "I *must* try to cooperate next time." Then she turned to me. "So, what happened to Craig?"

Annemarie Nevins Vale looked from Emma to me, and a little smile appeared at the corners of her lips. I've never struck a woman. Of course, until that moment, I'd never had any desire to do so. But it suddenly occurred to me how easy it would be to lean across the coffee table and punch her in the jaw . . .

I restrained myself.

"He's dead, Emma," I said. "I'm sure of it. Last Saturday, after your crash on the Brooklyn Bridge, he took off in the borrowed Town Car. He probably came directly here, parking right about where Chap and I are parked now. He waited while Annemarie did her concerned-stepmother routine at the hospital. That night, when Walter was asleep upstairs, she slipped out and met him here. And that's when she killed him.''

Mrs. Vale's perfect face gave nothing away, but Emma's face registered confusion.

''But why?'' she said. ''He could always try killing me again, and he and Sarah were about to be married, which is what she wanted. I'm sure she was planning to get rid of Craig later, like she did with Michael Trent, but why on earth would she kill him *now*?''

I smiled over at Emma. Excellent: she'd delivered the lines perfectly. I'd already told her and Stan all of this the night before at Amber's, but she was pulling a Meryl Streep now; ''setting the stage,'' to use her own phrase, the phrase she'd used when she'd surprised me by arriving here. Trying to get a rise out of Annemarie—which is precisely what I needed. Until the woman admitted something in the presence of witnesses, I was flying blind.

''Why kill him now, you ask?'' I said, smiling omnisciently at Emma while my mind raced, searching for the best possible answer. I had several theories. ''That's easy, Emma.'' *Think*, Joe, I commanded myself. Why the hell *did* she . . . unless . . .

''*Blackmail!*''

I'd blurted out the word before I even realized that I was speaking. Emma raised her hands to her bosom and gasped, which was probably not what Meryl Streep would have done. Fortunately, I wasn't looking at her. I was watching Annemarie. And in that split second after I shouted the word, she slipped. Her eyes widened and her lovely, red mouth fell open. Then, immediately, she regained her composure. Her hands tightened in her lap, and her eyes and lips once more became cold, contemptuous slits.

And I knew I had been correct.

I took a deep breath and said, ''Yes, blackmail. Craig Davis was a creep—you found that out yourself, Emma, and sent him on his way—but he may have had second thoughts about murder. Besides, he'd finally gotten one of the Vale girls to agree to marry him. He wasn't as desperate now as he was when Annemarie here first approached him with her charming suggestion. Yes, he waited here Saturday, in this very room. But when she arrived to dress him down for screwing up again, *she's* the one who got a surprise. He was reneging, backing out of the deal. He'd soon have his own meal ticket: he didn't have to risk his freedom by killing anybody. He was free and clear—but then he made his fatal mistake!''

I paused dramatically, looking expectantly over at Emma. She blinked. Then came the dawn, and Meryl Streep was with us once more.

"And what was his mistake?" she asked.

I pointed down at Annemarie. "He hit *her* up for money. To buy his silence. Otherwise, he'd go to the police. And she lost it. *That's* when she—"

"That's—when—I—*what*?!"

Annemarie Nevins Vale rose slowly to her feet, an expression of triumph on her face. We all stared at her. There was a flash of light against the curtains behind her, and into the sudden silence came a loud peal of thunder. She stared right back at us, her triumph growing into a dreadful smile.

"That's—when—I—*what*?!" she repeated. "What did I do *then*, Mr. Wilder? You seem to be so well informed: tell us all what I did. Did I shoot him, poison him, hit him over the head?" She jabbed a long, scarlet thumbnail in the direction of a side door. "Maybe he's hanging in the closet over there. Do you want to check it out? Honestly! I didn't kill him because I didn't see him, here or anywhere else. I didn't even *know* him!"

From the doorway, Chap Lannigan at last broke his long silence.

"You didn't know him?" he said softly, sounding clearly puzzled. "So, do you always fuck complete strangers on that couch over there?"

Annemarie whipped her head around, giving him a brief look that all but shouted HIRED HELP. Then she turned back to Emma and me. "Prove it! Prove *any* of this—this—this *fantastic* pack of lies! I didn't kill Laura or Michael Trent, and I have no idea where Craig Davis is. I'm sure he'll turn up eventually, and won't *you* feel like fools!" She crossed her arms and raised her chin victoriously, staring at me.

I stared right back. "No, we won't feel like fools. Because Craig isn't going to 'turn up eventually.' He isn't going to turn up at all—not alive, at any rate. And until he *does* turn up, *you* are in very serious trouble. Chap, call the Nassau County police."

Chap straightened up and stepped forward from the door. One step was all he got before her voice stopped him.

"Oh, yes, *Chap*—God, what a name!—by all means, call them. Get them here right now! Do you know what I'm going to tell them? The truth! I saw a light on out here in the poolhouse, so I got my husband's gun and came to investigate. I saw two dark figures—trespassers, prowlers, *thieves*, for all I knew—coming toward me. I thought they were going to harm me. I fired. End of story!"

I smiled, leaning down to crush out my cigarette in the big brass ashtray. "No, Mrs. Vale, that's not the end of the story." I turned to Chap. "Tell her to sit down."

"Sit down," Chap told her.

She sat down.

"My father doesn't believe in guns," Emma said. "He's certainly never owned one. As his wife, you should know that, Ann."

Mrs. Vale stared at her, the color slowly draining from her face.

"That's beside the point," I said. "There's a man in Tampa, Rod Hutchinson, who can identify you as Marie, the woman who brought Michael Trent to New York. I'm sure someone at the yacht club will remember that it was you who got him the job there. Dr. Nevins will probably remember whether or not you left your home in Syosset shortly before midnight on the night of Laura's murder. A bartender named Morty has an excellent memory for faces, and he remembers yours: he can link you romantically with Craig Davis as far back as four or five years ago. Arnold Jacobs, the proprietor of a Davis car dealership in Queens, and his employee, a young woman named Mindy, will tell the cops all about the Town Car *you* returned there after you killed Craig, the Town Car with all the interesting nicks and dents and scrapes of paint from Emma's car. Craig always made a big deal about thanking them when he re-turned the borrowed cars, but not this time. This time the car was left outside the gates, the keys slipped in the mail-box. If I have to call every taxi service in the tri-state area, I'll find the driver who picked you up outside the Davis dealership last weekend and brought you home. You wouldn't have dared to use your own chauffeur, but if you *did*, I'll get it out of him. And what about the phone calls? The one from Chap this morning, and the one I made to you from that phone right over there, telling you to come to the poolhouse if you didn't want me to go to the police. The phone company keeps records: both calls were logged somewhere. Chap made his call in front of two witnesses, and he spoke to a maid or a housekeeper before you came on the line. He heard what I said on the phone here: he was standing right next to me." No, he wasn't, but she didn't know that. "We'll both swear to it. Won't we, Chap?"

"We sure will, *Annemarie*," came the voice from the doorway. Then, softer: "God, what a name!"

She didn't bother to wither him with her glare this time. She was staring at me. Wary. Calculating. Planning her next move. I could see it in her eyes.

I didn't want to hear any more of what Annemarie Nev-ins Vale had to say. It's time, I reminded myself. It's time for all of this to stop.

"But none of this really matters, does it?" I concluded. "Whether or not we can prove any of this. Because, either way, you're screwed. What do you think Walter's going to do when he gets back from Tokyo? What do you think all your friends at the club and the charities and Masterson Electronics are going to do? Not to mention the gossip columns. By the time we're through with you, you'll *wish* you were in prison. You know, it's almost funny, Laura loving *Madame Bovary* so much, because she doesn't remind me of Madame Bovary. *You* do. The middle-class girl married to a nice, respectable, middle-class dentist, with a nice house in Syosset. But you want more. You ingratiate your way into Laura Vale's world, and you immediately start planning. You don't just want to hang out with Laura Vale: you want to *be* her. Rich? That isn't enough, not for the likes of you. You want to be *stinking* rich. You want to be Laura Vale rich! So you plot and you plan and you scheme—''

"Oh, *really*, Mr. Wilder—'' she began.

"*Shut up*! You get your sleazy beach boys and penniless rich boys to do your killing for you, and then you kill *them*. All so you can be Ann Vale, the big, rich society woman. Well, not anymore. When I'm finished bending his ear, Walter Vale will be through with you. And you needn't expect alimony, either. He'll cut you off with nothing, and if you complain he'll start a police investigation. Something will be found to prove all this: it always is. And even if it isn't, you lose, anyway. Prison! You'll be in prison, all right. Shunned. Ostracized. *Broke*! You needn't bother going back to Dr. Nevins: he's already forgotten you. And you're getting a little long in the tooth, you know. Pretty soon, you won't even be able to seduce another larcenous lifeguard. What will you do *then*, Annemarie? Well, there's always Forty-second Street. You're probably not qualified to do much else. Some great woman *you* turned out to be! Some lady of the manor! Hell, you're so unobtrusive, so negligible, so *unimportant*, nobody even bothered to tell me who you *were*! I had to figure it out for myself. Emma didn't tell me that Annemarie Nevins and Ann Vale were the same person because it never occurred to her to do so. That's the impression you make on people, you *anonymous* creature!''

There was a long silence as she and I stared at each other. Slowly, a change came into her face. It was subtle, but it was there: defeat. But I had no time to gloat. The silence was broken by Emma's low, appreciative whistle.

''Wow!'' she said. ''That was some speech! But tell me, Joe, how did you figure it out?''

Then I made my big mistake, the one that could have cost all our lives. I looked away from Mrs. Vale. I turned to Emma, smiling, and told her the truth.

''I didn't,'' I said. ''I'm a writer, you see, and it was the most logical scenario. As a matter of fact—''

The scream cut me off. It began as a low growl and rose in volume as it rose in pitch, becoming a long, deafening wail of rage. Annemarie Nevins Vale shot forward out of the armchair and snatched up the big, heavy brass ashtray with both hands. She turned and hurled it at Chap. He dropped the gun to the floor and brought up his hands in front of him. I never saw the impact: Mrs. Vale grabbed the edge of the coffee table and overturned it. The opposite edge smashed into my shins, and it must have hit Emma, as well. The two of us went flying backward onto the couch behind us. With a loud thud, the coffee table came down on its side before us. Chap fell back against the door as the brass ashtray crashed down to the floor.

Still the screaming continued. I saw a blur of blue raincoat and maroon pantsuit as Mrs. Vale threw her body across the room toward the doorway, landing on her hands and knees at Chap's feet. In a flash, she had the gun in her hand.

I grabbed Emma and shoved her down onto the floor behind the coffee table, then I dived down on top of her. I held her tightly, covering her body with my own, and waited for the gunshots.

There was only one. It didn't seem as loud as before, I

don't know why. Expectation, I guess. Just the one small explosion, followed by an ominous silence. It hadn't hit me, and it hadn't hit Emma. Oh, God, I thought, *Chap*! I was about to move when the silence was broken.

"Okay," Chap said from the other side of the coffee table, the other side of the world. "It's over."

I let go of Emma, rolled off of her, and rose to my knees. Chap still stood in the doorway, his face and clothing covered with cigarette ashes. He was looking down at the floor near his feet. I followed his gaze with my own.

Emma moaned softly as she sat up on the floor. "What the hell happened? What—"

I turned on my knees and grasped her shoulders, blocking her view, pressing her face against my chest. I buried my face in her damp, sweet-smelling blond hair. I heard Chap moving over to the telephone, and I heard his low voice giving instructions to the police. After a few moments, I heard the soft sounds Emma made as she wept for her mother, Laura Vale, whose presence I no longer felt in this room. But most of all I heard the silence, the awful, final silence of death. And gradually, beyond that silence, I heard the other sounds, the sounds that were coming from outside: the rain and the wind and the thunder of that dark and stormy night.

SEVENTEEN

Jenny Makes Her Mind Up

The next day, Saturday, the rain was gone. The sky above Long Island looked ragged, drained, and the water in the Sound was choppy and gray. As the afternoon progressed, the remaining clouds dispersed and the sun grew stronger. The sky and the water gradually turned from gray to deep, clear blue. It ended up being quite a lovely day. Well, visually, at any rate.

After the police and the paramedics had been and gone the night before, Chap took Emma back to the city, but I remained on Long Island. I checked into a hotel in Oyster Bay and fell into bed, exhausted. I wasn't able to sleep long, though. At nine o'clock in the morning, I was back at the Masterson/Vale place, talking to the police on the lawn outside the poolhouse.

I told them the whole story as I knew it, and then I watched through the big picture window as four people, three men and a woman, went over the entire interior of the place. It took them less than an hour to find the poker with the traces of relatively fresh blood on the hooked end. Samples were taken and rushed away in a van. Not long after that, one of the forensic people thought to look in the

big bin at the side of the building, where the pool equipment was stored. More bloodstains were found there, a few
drops on the wooden floor under a big chlorine container.
More bagging and labeling ensued.

I was wandering around the grounds about an hour later,
frowning at the vulgar statues and admiring the stamina of
whoever kept the grass so neatly trimmed, when I noticed a
great deal of activity. The woman from the forensic team
came running up the steps from the beach, calling to her colleagues. They—and I—followed her down to a sturdy boat-
house near the base of the steps. The Vales kept two boats in
there, a medium-sized powerboat and a small, lightweight
aluminum craft, a dinghy, with a little outboard motor. It was
this smaller one that was now the subject of everyone's scrutiny. More blood, in a couple of cracks near a seam under the
single bench. Out came the bags and the labels.

I left them to their grisly work and went back up the
stone steps to the patio behind the main house. I looked up:
two women in black uniform dresses and white aprons were
watching me from the wrought iron balcony outside an upstairs bedroom. One of them was clutching an old-
fashioned feather duster in her hands. I waved to them.
They blushed and giggled and went back inside the house.
I turned around on the patio and looked out over the Sound.

How far did she get? I wondered. She'd been traced from
the poker to the storage bin, and then—days later, I imagine,
after Walter had left for Japan—she'd stolen out of the house
in the dead of night to finish the job. She dragged the body
from the bin, across the lawn, and down the steps to the boat-
house. She must have wrapped him in something, some plastic covering that would have gone overboard with him.
Assuming that it was very late at night, and that the moving
of a very tall, two-hundred-plus-pound body had reasonably
exhausted her, how far out would she have gone?

I stared out over the water, wondering where Craig's body
was, until a uniformed officer came to fetch me. I was driven
in a squad car through the front gates and past the news vans

that had materialized there, to a police station in Oyster Bay. There, in a room with three officials and a pretty young stenographer, I told the whole story again, in the form of a statement. By the time I got back to my rental car in the lane near the side wall of the estate, it was nearly dusk.

Then, as the sun was setting, I drove back to the city, to my apartment on Hudson Street. To my life.

Early Sunday morning, a flight from Tokyo arrived at Kennedy Airport. I wasn't there, but Jenny and Rachel Cohen were, and Jenny told me all about it later.

Walter Vale was alone, having left his traveling companions in Japan to finish the deal they'd all been working on. He looked very tired, Jenny said, which was to be expected, all things considered. Tired and sad. But he brightened considerably when he came through Customs and found his two daughters and Sarah Masterson waiting for him. Stan Smith was there, too, with a fresh bandage on his right temple. There was much embracing and kissing and weeping. I know that for a fact: I saw the photos in the newspapers, and there was a short video clip of the event on that night's six o'clock news.

Ignoring the hundred shouted questions and the flash cameras and microphones thrust in their direction, the family made their way through the crowd to the waiting limousine. Jenny and Rachel followed them in Rachel's car, and when they got to the apartment on Fifth Avenue, the two friends remained for a lunch that nobody ate and coffee that soon grew cold in Mrs. Masterson's living room. Rachel and the housekeeper stayed by the constantly ringing telephones, offering crisp "No comment"'s to everyone who called. Jenny sat with the family, offering condolences and small talk until she was sure that any initial awkwardness in the formerly estranged group had passed. Before she and Rachel finally departed, they heard Walter announce to his daughters and his mother-in-law that he would put the Oyster Bay estate up for sale and take a

house in town, near his family. Everyone agreed that this
was a good idea.

I'm told that I was the subject of a brief discussion, and
Mrs. Masterson and Emma asked Jenny to thank me. I understand I am to be celebrated with gifts and dinner parties,
and I have already received a nice note from Mrs. Masterson. I don't expect that the dinner parties will be any time
soon, of course, which is fine with me. Now it's time for
that family to mourn, and to mend.

And perhaps they will. As Jenny was leaving Mrs. Masterson's that afternoon, she noticed something she'd never
seen before, not in all the years she'd known Emma Vale
Smith. Emma was sitting on a couch beside her younger
sister, and the two women were holding hands. Walter sat
near his daughters, and the three of them were talking quietly. That was how Jenny left them there; saddened, subdued, close together, straining to reach across the chasm
that had separated them.

Three days later, Wednesday, I received a telephone call
from St. Thomas that I'd been half-expecting for several
weeks. The caller was Austin Hammond, the Virgin Islands–based lawyer who had been my missing friend's law
partner. He told me that he was flying to New York that
weekend, and he asked me to meet him the following Monday afternoon at an address on Park Avenue. At that time,
he informed me, we would be signing all the necessary
papers.

The Mongoose Fund was a reality.

I sat for a long time that day after hanging up the phone,
remembering my friend, and everyone else in St. Thomas,
and the strange series of events that had led, years later, to
this eventuality. Then, when I didn't want to think about it
anymore, I went back to the phone and called Stan Smith
at his office on Wall Street.

We spoke for twenty minutes or so, and Stan assured me
that he would take very good care of me. I asked after

Emma, and he told me that she and her sister were off somewhere, pricing bassinets. We laughed about that.

When I was finished with Stan, I made two more phone calls.

It has been called the most beautiful residential block in New York City, and it's easy to see why. The short stretch of Morton Street between Hudson and Bedford has wide white sidewalks lined with tall, graceful trees. The buildings are mostly small, three- or four-story townhouses that date from times when beauty was an architectural consideration. They are painted deep, warm colors, and they are graced with flower boxes and rounded bay windows and gleaming black wrought-iron fire escapes. There is a slight curve in the street, in the middle of the block, and the rows of houses on either side follow it. The quiet, Old World place is actually laid out in the shape of a gentle smile, which is entirely appropriate. On a late afternoon in March, when the lights in the windows are just beginning to come on and the shadows of the bare trees are lengthening, it has everything to smile about.

We stood in the center of the big, empty front room, the four of us, looking around. It was on the ground floor of a brownstone in the center of the block, which is actually seven steps up from the street. Four stories, all told: a three-story residence with a separate basement apartment. The room we were in, the biggest in the building, had a polished wood floor and a bay window and—yes!—a working fireplace. There was an archway three quarters of the way back, separating the rear section as a dining area. Behind that was the kitchen, with its gleaming new fixtures, butcher-block center island, and a door leading out to— yes!—a tiny, fenced-in backyard. The big front rooms on the second and third stories could become an office and a master bedroom, I imagined. The back room on the second floor could be a guest room, and the rear section of the top floor could be, with a little renovation, the bathroom of my dreams. Of course, you'd have to knock out the existing bathroom up there, but . . .

As if reading my thoughts, Mrs. Wahlberg, the realtor, said, "Bathrooms on each floor—and one in the basement, of course. You could rent that out, if you wanted. This place is four blocks from NYU, and half the students and faculty are looking for basement apartments . . ."

"Yes," I said.

Then it was Jenny's turn. "This fireplace is gorgeous— and twice the size of the one in your place on Hudson Street. The backyard is just big enough for a table and chairs . . ."

"Yes," I said.

Mrs. Wahlberg again: "The quietest block in New York, as well as the prettiest. And you'd have an excellent market and an excellent dry cleaner right around the corner—but I suppose you know that. You live three blocks from here."

I was tired of saying yes, so I made a sound like, "Hmmm . . ." Then I went over to the bay window. I sat in the old-fashioned window seat and gazed down at the tree-lined, movie-set street outside. The sun was setting, and a little breeze rustled the bare branches. An elderly woman was walking a collie on the sidewalk across the street, and the dog was exploring the trees appreciatively. A boy and a girl, perhaps sixteen, came out of a house a few doors down and walked away, hand in hand, toward the avenue. A young woman marched briskly by in front of the window, all clicking heels and bouncing blond hair and shiny leather coat. She reminded me of Emma Vale Smith . . .

"Joe?" Jenny had come quietly over to stand behind me.

I smiled up at her, then looked back at the view. "Look out there, Jenny. What do you see?"

She smiled, too, remembering. "I see the world."

"Yes," I said. "So do I." I turned back to her. "Do you remember what I asked you that day?"

"I remember."

I nodded. I looked beyond her. Chap Lannigan leaned against the mantel at the fireplace, watching us, waiting. Mrs. Wahlberg had wandered discreetly back to the dining area. She wasn't watching us, but I knew that she was waiting, too.

"It's a beautiful house," Jenny said. "And with the— the fund, you can certainly afford it—"

"Yes, I can afford it," I said. "Especially if I rent the basement . . ." I smiled again.

She eyed me suspiciously. "What are you thinking, Joe?"

I didn't say anything, but I inclined my head, indicating Chap over at the mantel. He couldn't hear us, but he scowled at us as if he could. He knew we were discussing him.

"Ohhhh . . . yes," she said, nodding. We were both thinking about the drab room on East Sixth Street. "Yes, the basement would be perfect. So, are you going to take it?"

I looked back out at the street. "I can't answer your question, because *you* haven't answered *my* question. You know what I want to do. If you'll help me, if you'll be a part of it, I'll consider this place an investment. A *business* investment. You understand?"

"The Mongoose Fund," she whispered.

"Yes," I said. "The Mongoose Fund. I'll only use the fund for this house if we're in business. I'll offer Chap and you permanent salaries for what will amount to part-time work, and he can have the basement, if he wants it. I'll take the rent out of his salary."

"I don't think he'll say no to that," she said.

"Neither do I," I agreed. Then I called over to him. "Hey, Chap, what do you think of this place?"

He looked around the room, then back at me. "I could get used to it."

I nodded and turned back to Jenny. I did not tell her that I'd already offered him the job and that he'd accepted it.

She studied me. "What if *I* say no?"

I shrugged. "I'll go ahead with my plan, anyway—but

I won't buy a house. I'll just stay where I am on Hudson Street, I guess. But if I have partners, I mean, if this is definitely a business venture, I'll definitely need a bigger place.'' I smiled at her again. ''I know this sounds like a song, but—well, it all depends on you.''

Now she was staring out the window, and a faraway look came into her face. I waited, aware that Mrs. Wahlberg would be wanting to get home to dinner. I was hungry, myself. And I knew, the way you know these things, that I was going to take Jenny and Chap out to dinner, no matter what she decided. The restaurant was nearby, the one where Jenny and I had met three weeks ago. The one that had the *poulet avec artichaud*. I love artichokes.

Jenny blinked and turned from the view to look down at me again.

''I was just thinking,'' she said. ''About Emma. And about St. Thomas seven years ago . . .''

I nodded. ''I've been thinking about them, too.''

We looked at each other for a long moment.

Then, almost imperceptibly, she nodded. She took a deep breath and turned around to face the others.

''Mrs. Wahlberg,'' she called. ''I think Joe has something to say to you.''

Mrs. Wahlberg came back into the room, a little anticipatory smile forming on her lips. ''Have you come to a decision?''

I stood up from the window seat and went over to her.

''Yes,'' I said, ''I've come to a decision. I'll take it.'' I looked over my shoulder at the man who watched from the fireplace and the woman who watched from the window. Then I turned back to the realtor. ''*We'll* take it.''